A Place for Us

a Blue Harbor novel

OLIVIA MILES

Rosewood Press

A Place for Us

1

The call came on Monday afternoon when Britt Conway should have been just returning to her obsessively organized desk overlooking the Chicago River, a salad from her favorite lunch spot across the street from her office building in hand for when she had time to eat it, which she rarely did because she usually got so caught up with her never-ending task list.

Instead, she was conveniently just getting out of her less than reliable shower, cranky from the lack of hot water that was an ongoing issue in the vintage apartment building that had seemed so charming upon first inspection, her unemployment status now treading dangerously into the four-week mark. Panic level? Escalating, and curbed only slightly by the promise of a job interview on Wednesday.

She checked the screen, hoping it was the recruiter who had promised to be in touch this week, and knew at once that it was bad news, because she had an intuition for these sorts of things. Her guard was always up, her mind wandering to worst-case scenarios, because she'd never quite let herself relax, no matter how much meditation she did or long, not-so-steamy showers she took, or miles she ran.

She'd run four hundred miles away from her

hometown fourteen years ago, after all, and yet here she was, palms sweating, heart racing, staring at her sister's name on the screen, afraid to answer.

"What happened?" she asked, and when Amelia didn't laugh off Britt's worry the way she might have done other times, she felt her stomach roil.

"It's Dad," Amelia said, and then Britt really did feel it. Full force. A wave of emotions that she couldn't even register because they were rolling over her all at once, making it difficult to breathe. Fear was top of the list, of course. But guilt…so much guilt.

"He's fine," Amelia added quickly, and Britt felt a breath escape that she hadn't even realized she had been holding. "But he was standing on the ladder. You know, the top step that you aren't even supposed to stand on? The one that comes with a big warning sign telling you not to step on that step?"

Britt knew. She had a clear memory of her mother warning her father not to go so high each year when he tacked Christmas lights to their roofline. "He never heeded that advice," she said ruefully.

"Nope! And he fell, of course. Broke his left forearm and his left shin. He's lucky he didn't break his neck!"

"Don't even say such things," Britt warned, but she was smiling just the same. In relief. Two broken bones. He would live. And hopefully learn a lesson, too. "What was he doing standing on a ladder like that? At his age!"

"He's only sixty," Amelia reminded her. She sighed, and Britt could hear the noises from a hospital in the background. "Still. He's not as young as he once was, but try telling him that! He was reaching for some extra bushels. The ones that he stores up in the loft of the west barn?"

The loft in the west barn had been used as storage space for as long as Conway Orchard had been around. Had it been a traditional barn, there may have been hay to cushion the fall, but their family was in the business of fruit and wine, not horses and livestock.

"And down he went!" Amelia continued. Britt could picture her tossing her hands in her air. No doubt poor Dennis Conway had already been lectured at length by his second oldest daughter. Britt almost felt sorry for the guy—if she wasn't so mad at the worry he'd caused her. "Now the doctors are saying he's off work until the arm cast comes off in a month, and of course Steve has a vacation planned that can't be canceled..."

Britt had the uneasy feeling that they hadn't quite reached the point of the call.

"And I'm busy at the café, and Maddie's busy helping me, of course. And I can't be short-staffed, not with the summer season! And Cora has her shop to run. And, well, he's asking for you."

Britt closed her eyes. In all these years, her father had never asked for her. He'd let her go because he knew that was what she had needed to do. And now she was in no position to turn down his request. She clutched the phone tighter in her hand and braced herself. "What is he asking?"

"You need to come home, Britt," Amelia said.

Home. Britt heaved a sigh. She supposed deep down she knew that she couldn't dodge it forever.

A PLACE FOR US

*

For many people, Blue Harbor was a destination point, a summer vacation spot, the place where they returned year after year to stroll the Main Street shops or pick cherries or swim in the cool waters of Lake Huron. For those people, the small, northern Michigan town conjured up images of ice cream cones, and ferry rides to the ever quaint Evening Island, and street fests and long, lazy, sun-filled days.

For Britt Conway, it stirred up no such memories. For her, thinking of her hometown put a knot in her stomach, and right now, as she crossed the town line and the crisp red barn that was the hallmark of her family's orchard came into view in the distance, she felt downright queasy.

It might have been the bagel she'd eaten for breakfast, she told herself. Or the ice cream she'd consumed for dinner last night, after the pizza, of course, because really, how was she supposed to even think about cooking for herself when she had to pack, and plan, and…dread.

And the tears that burned her eyes and blurred her vision: allergies. It was all this fresh air and nature. She turned up the air-conditioning. That should do it.

Except that it didn't. And the closer she came to the neat rows of fruit trees that went on for acres and acres, as far as the eye could see, the more she struggled to blink away her pain.

Conway Orchard had been in her family for three generations. Her grandfather had started it as a local produce supplier, planting the cherry trees that were common in the region along with apples and pears. When her father and his brother took over the daily operations, they bought the neighboring farm and expanded their crop to include berries and grapes that could thrive in a colder climate, which they soon turned into wine that was bottled and sold along with cider and the pies that her mother sold fresh every Sunday at their market.

Britt could still taste those pies if she closed her eyes, but like this town, she'd tried to push those memories aside. Some things were better forgotten because they just hurt too much to think about.

With a sigh, she pulled her car to a stop in the gravel parking lot and checked her reflection in the rearview mirror. Really, she was stalling. Delaying the inevitable surge of emotions that just kept coming and had been since she'd left Chicago this morning.

Still, she reminded herself. She had nothing better to do at the moment. She may as well be useful. And three weeks helping out on the orchard might keep her busy enough to stop worrying about what came next in her future, because if there was one thing that made Britt more uneasy than being in Blue Harbor, it was uncertainty.

It was a warm day for June, and she knew that her father would be pleased about that. Nothing made the man grumble more than the fickleness of the weather. It was one of the things that had made her twitch growing up here; the lack of predictability. The lack of control. Life was so much easier when you could see the problem and face it head on. But her father liked the challenge, he said, and she supposed that she'd gotten some of that from him, despite their other differences.

Now, as she walked across the gravel path that separated the numerous buildings on the property, her heart started to pick up speed despite the dread that had made her sluggish since she'd received her sister Amelia's call. She hadn't seen her father or sisters in years, even though she called often, and promised to visit, even if she always found an excuse not to.

She bypassed the building closest to the street, which served as a tasting room and market, and went straight for the largest of the three barns in the back, where the business offices were housed.

Inside, it smelled of fruit, sweet and aromatic, bringing her back to happier times, times spent taste-testing her father's newest blends, and coming up with names for their shiny labels. There was a year for each of his children's births, and Uncle Steve's three daughters too, her namesake being the oldest. The vintage.

Her father wouldn't be at work, she knew this much, but she wanted to take a look around, familiarize herself with what he'd been up to before she went home.

Really, she knew that she was just procrastinating until it could no longer be avoided.

She knocked on the open door to her father's office, grinning when her Uncle Steve looked up from a stack of papers and pulled his reading glasses from his face. "Britt? Is that you? Well, aren't you a sight!"

Her eyes teared up as he crossed the room and pulled her into a hug. A few years older than her father, he'd stepped out of retirement to come back to the farm for the week, she knew.

Now she saw that he was grey in the temple and a little thin in the face. She tried to calculate how long it had been since she'd seen him and realized with a wave of guilt that it had been five years, and brief, in and out for her cousin's wedding, which hadn't lasted much longer than it took to drive back over the state line.

"How are Gabby, Brooke, and Jenna?" She hadn't kept in good touch with her cousins, even though they'd been as close as sisters once. But then, she hadn't done a very good job at keeping in touch with her sisters either.

Work kept her busy. Until it didn't. And now...Well, now she was where she was needed until she figured out her next step.

"Oh, they're fine. Brooke is still away, but Gabby and Jenna will no doubt want to fill you in on all their news themselves. You girls can talk all night long, as I seem to recall." His eyes twinkled at the memory, and Britt felt something in her soften.

She could remember countless sleepovers, some in bedrooms, some in living rooms, some in tents in the backyard, with all the girls huddled under blankets, looking up into the clear night sky, hoping to catch a glimpse of the Northern Lights that could sometimes be seen to the lucky ones who waited. The younger girls always fell asleep first, frustrated with themselves the next morning, even if there hadn't been anything to see. But Britt always held out, hoping to see something elusive and special. Knowing just how precious every moment was.

"It's good to have you back," Steve said, squeezing her shoulder. "Even if I wish the circumstances were different."

For a moment, she thought he was referring to her losing her job, but no one in Blue Harbor knew about that, and she intended to keep it that way. Work was a good excuse to get in and get out.

"That was one heck of a fall," Britt commented now, pulling back. "It was good of you to step in until I got here." Yes, it was Friday, she had pushed things off a few days, claiming a work project had to be wrapped up, when really, she had to sit through that rather unpromising job interview, and then…Well, then she really did need all of Thursday to pack and mentally prepare for this return visit. She hadn't been back properly since…

Her heart squeezed tight. She trained her eyes on her uncle. Work. She would work as hard as she could for the next three weeks until her father was out of his arm cast and on crutches.

"That's what family is for," Uncle Steve said, and Britt pushed back the wave of guilt that reared strong and steady. "It was good of you to come all the way up here to help. I'd stick around myself if your aunt hadn't already booked that cruise for tomorrow." He shook his head. "Terrible timing."

"Nonsense. You deserve that trip. And I had some time off…" More like all the time in the world, she thought.

"Well, you won't be alone," Steve said briskly. "Your father had the sense to hire a manager last year when I stepped aside from the business."

Britt frowned. "He never mentioned that." Shame bit at her when she considered how their phone calls usually went, and how infrequently they spoke at all. When they did, they often chatted about her job or her sisters. He was vague about the family business, and she suspected that he didn't want to hear her advice. She may be a management consultant, but she was still his little girl, and her father was... Stubborn, she thought, her lips pursing again when she thought of the top step of that ladder.

"No? Never?" Steve scratched the corner of his chin. "I assumed he would have mentioned that to you."

Was it just her, or did something seem to pass through Steve's eyes? Something like...panic?

"No," Britt said, shaking her head. "I assumed that he was running it all on his own." There were eight full-time employees who oversaw everything from the market to the pruning to the daily tours, to the pressing and bottling of the ciders and wines. With a boss who treated them like family, there was little turnover, and she'd assumed that he had all the support he needed.

"Well, he should be able to fill you in and, um, help you out." Steve struggled to meet her eye as he turned and shuffled a few papers on the desk.

There was a knock on the door behind her and Steve's eyes opened in surprise. "And there he is now. Britt, you remember Robbie."

She stared at her uncle, her mouth, she was sure, resembling something eerily close to the fish she and her cousins used to catch on her family's dock. *Remember* Robbie? How could she ever forget Robbie? Her first love. Her first heartbreak.

Her only love. And her *last* heartbreak, she told herself firmly.

Only Robbie was long gone, out in Boston.

Surely, her uncle was mistaken.

Still, her mouth went dry as she turned around and locked eyes with him. Dark eyes. Wavy hair. Hard body. Robbie Bradford.

He may not have been the reason she'd left Blue Harbor, but he was certainly one of the reasons she'd stayed away.

And if she'd known that he was here, on her property, working for her family's business, she most certainly never would have come back.

*

This day just kept getting worse. It had started when he forgot Keira's stuffed bear for show and tell, even though that was probably technically her responsibility. It was a teaching moment, he knew, but the tears of disappointment that shone in her eyes had torn at his heartstrings, and he'd done what he knew he shouldn't have and turned the car around, went back for Mr. Bear, and then had no choice but to physically walk his daughter into the school building, rather than drop her off as he usually did, to join the others in lines on the playground.

He'd tried to keep it brief, tried to quickly sign her in as tardy (again) and say good-bye, not allowing his eyes to drift anywhere near the nurse's office door. But like all good intentions, it didn't work out in his favor. While Keira scampered off with her bear in hand, he just missed the opportunity of a quick getaway when Carly Patterson (or "Nurse Carly" as she liked to be called) appeared in her doorway, her blue eyes a little too bright for his liking, her smile a bit too suggestive.

Had he seen the signs for the festival, she'd asked coyly, and he didn't have the heart to tell her that no one in Blue Harbor was unaware of the summer festival. It was an annual tradition at the end of each June, and even if it wasn't, the signs for it were all over town.

Still, he'd grunted some form of a response, enough to assure her that he would, in fact, be there, enough to make her eyes light up as she disappeared back into her office, wiggling her fingers in goodbye.

He'd kept his head bent as he'd strode back to the front door, past Lauren Mackenzie at the front desk, another classmate from his youth, who was staring at him a little too keenly.

He wasn't interested in these women. He wasn't interested in dating. He'd been in love before and he'd learned his lesson.

Yet here he was, being schooled again. Britt Conway, looking as pretty as she had the last time he'd seen her.

Nearly half a lifetime ago.

"Robbie, Britt's here to help out until Dennis is back on his feet," he heard a voice say, pulling his eyes away from Britt, snapping him from the shock of being in the same room as her again.

Robbie darted his gaze at Steve Conway, watching the way the man shifted nervously on his feet. So he'd known. And decided not to say anything. And here Robbie had dared to think that he'd stepped out of retirement to take over for a few weeks. Surely he was going to reschedule that cruise?

"Well, I'll leave you kids to it," Steve said now, as he fumbled for his reading glasses and pushed past Robbie for the door. He turned and looked at Britt. "It's good to have you back, Britt."

Back. She was back. Robbie still couldn't quite process those words.

Steve dropped his glasses and bent to pick them up, and then, with one more glance in both of their directions, he was gone, leaving Robbie alone with a woman he hadn't intended to see again, not when he moved back to Blue Harbor, not even when he'd taken the job at Conway Farms. Other than a wedding a few years back, and then only for a single night at an inn two towns over, Britt hadn't been back in fourteen years, they'd all said, not since her mother had died.

Fourteen years was a long time. And Robbie knew better than most people how deep a loss could cut you, change you.

He offered her a smile. Rolled back on his heels, trying to think of what to even say. I'm sorry? Are you sorry? How are you? Why are you here?

There were many things he could ask Britt Conway, after all, but none of that seemed to be his place anymore. And besides, he'd changed. He wasn't the same boy she knew all those years ago. And looking at her, with her blond hair pulled back in a tight knot, not a strand out of place, and her grey eyes looking wan and cool instead of bright and alive, she wasn't the same girl either.

"This is a surprise," he said, resting his hand on the knob of the open door, preparing for a quick exit.

She raised a single eyebrow. "So you weren't tipped off?"

Ah, so she was still mad at him, then. Why, he couldn't be sure.

After all, last he'd checked, she'd been the one to break his heart, not the other way around.

2

Robbie pulled up to town hall and glanced at the clock on the dashboard of his truck. Keira's ballet recital was scheduled to start in fifteen minutes, and he hoped that his parents had gotten there ahead of time to save him a seat. It was bad enough picking her up from dance class each week when the single mothers decided to offer their services. Services described as offering to help with Keira's bun, because apparently he wasn't doing it correctly, or so the dance instructor, an older, strict, and severely thin woman who had been running the place for forty years, had told him, both verbally, and in a letter that she folded into Keira's pink tote bag.

Then there were the other offers: playdates at the park together, a seat at their holiday table, a carpooling schedule that he suspected would lead to more trouble than it was worth.

There was only one girl for him right now, and she was six.

With that, he grabbed the flowers he'd picked up for her at the flower shop and walked up the steps of the town hall to the auditorium that housed all community events, from the local theatre group to dance recitals.

The room was already crowded and buzzing, and he

scanned it quickly before spotting his mother, waving eagerly at him. He grinned to himself. Should have known they'd find a way to get the front row, center. He didn't need to ask how early they'd had to arrive to secure that spot. One of the perks of having a loyal staff at the inn they'd run all their married life, they told him.

Sometimes, he didn't know how he would have made it through the past year if they hadn't insisted he move back to town so they could help him out. As it was, he was in over his head most days, and he was already afraid of the teen years. And the tween years, which seemed like a new concept to him, and one that already made his stomach tighten when he thought of how close they were. Keira's birthday was coming up, just a couple of weeks away. It would be the second birthday they would spend without Stephanie.

And it still didn't sit right. He didn't know if it ever would.

Sometimes, he thought Keira had adjusted better than he had to this new arrangement, to leaving behind the city and coming to this small town. She was sweet, and at nearly seven, she was still happy to hold his hand, content to spend the weekends together. Happy to be his number one gal. His only gal.

"Thanks for getting her ready for this," he said to his mother, as he took his seat.

Bonnie gave him a reassuring smile. "I took extra care with the bun, although never having had a daughter, I'll admit that one of the mothers did have to assist me when I dropped her off backstage."

Robbie stifled a groan. Here it came. If it wasn't one of the unmarried or divorced women in town, it was his own mother. Everyone knew what was best for him. Or so they thought.

"A very nice woman," Bonnie continued, her eyes taking on a hopeful look. "All on her own, too. Said her husband left her and her little girl when the baby was only two!" She clucked. "She moved back to Blue Harbor from the Detroit area. Wanted a sense of community for her child. She takes the ferry over to Evening Island every day. Works at the big hotel over there. A good position, too." Bonnie gave a little smile.

"And she just volunteered all of this?" Robbie raised an eyebrow. He knew who his mother was referring to. It was Natalie Clark, who also happened to be Steve Conway's niece, on his wife's side. A conflict of interest in his opinion, and one that suited him just fine.

"Well, we got to chatting, while she helped with Keira's hair." His mother sniffed in defense. Then, because she couldn't help herself, she added, "She's a pretty woman, and I remember how now. One of the Clark girls. Such pretty blue eyes!"

"Mom." Robbie's tone was a warning, and because it wasn't the first time, he didn't need to elaborate.

Still, his mother's eyes popped in mock innocence. "What? I was just stating a fact. She has very pretty eyes."

Natalie did have pretty eyes. Robbie was not immune to this fact. He also wasn't oblivious to the fact that she was interested in dating him. And that clearly, his mother would be thrilled by this.

He was happy that the lights were dimming and the curtain was opening. The music started from the corner of the room, where Jenna Conway sat at a baby grand piano.

At the sight of Britt's cousin (and technically, Natalie's too, given that Jenna was Steve and Miriam's daughter) Robbie shifted in his seat, feeling agitated. Steve should have warned him that Britt was coming back after all this time. He supposed he should have expected it, bumping into her some time, when he'd moved back to town last spring. But word around town was that Britt had only returned once since she'd left town at the age of eighteen, and by then, he'd given up waiting around for her.

Robbie forced his attention on the stage as the music shifted and a parade of little girls in pale purple dresses that sparkled and shone took their spots, after much confusion that had the audience, himself included, laughing under their breath.

Near the middle, on the left, was Keira, her hair perfect, he had to admit, her makeup causing her cheeks to look rosier than usual. She caught his eye and grinned, and just for that moment, for that one perfect moment, his heart was so full that nothing else mattered.

Not that she didn't have a mother anymore. Not that he'd had to give up his life and come back to the town he'd tried to leave behind, all those years ago. Not to the fact that the girl who'd gotten away, whom he'd tried to forget and thought he had, was back.

And that now, she was all that he could think about.

A PLACE FOR US

*

Britt slowed to a stop as she turned onto Water Street and saw her childhood home come into view at the end of the road. It was the same white, Victorian-style home that she'd lived in every day of her first eighteen years. The same house where she and her sisters would sit on the porch in the summer, drinking lemonade and chatting first about toys and games, and later, clothes and makeup, and eventually, boys. The same house where her mother could be found in the kitchen at the back, baking pies from the fruit they grew on the farm.

The same house where her mother sat them all down and told them the worst news of their lives.

She'd avoided coming back here, into this house, since the day she'd left it. Avoided the reality of knowing that this time, when she went inside, her mother would not be standing at the big kitchen island, peeling apples or rolling out a pie crust. That her apron would be hung on the hook on the back of the pantry door. Or worse, that it might not be there at all.

A honk of a car horn behind her made her jump and she glanced up at her rearview mirror to see her sister Cora waving at her, her smile broad and impatient.

Well. She supposed she was at a full stop in the middle of the road, even if these roads were rarely busy.

Seeing no way around it now, she eased off the brake and pulled into the gravel driveway, careful to leave enough space for her second-youngest sister. She stepped out in the cool, early evening air, the sound of the water lapping at the shore calming her slightly.

Cora jumped out of the car, her auburn hair—the same shade as their father's—flying behind her in a ponytail, and Britt had barely stepped out of her own vehicle before she was enveloped in a hug. Like always, Cora smelled of cinnamon and cloves, even though it was June. One of the hazards of owning a year-round holiday shop, Britt supposed.

"I can't believe you're actually here," Cora said, blinking quickly.

"Of course I'm here," Britt said, wondering if her sister picked up on the defensive edge that had crept into her tone. Really, Cora's comment was fair. More than fair. It was Britt, perhaps, who hadn't been the fair one, fleeing the nest, leaving her younger sisters to keep living the life that she couldn't bear to face.

She glanced up at the house and back to Cora. "How's he doing?"

Cora nodded earnestly. "Good, I think. Maddie's been visiting him most, and Amelia brings him food every day from the café."

Britt nodded. Of course, they were all doing their part. She was right to have come.

"And—" Here, Cora began blinking, a little too rapidly for Britt's liking. "And there's a caregiver that helps him. That was Amelia's doing. I think she felt guilty that she couldn't be here every day, and there's a great service—"

"Sounds like a good idea to me," Britt said. After all, none of them had any medical experience, and it sounded like she was going to be kept busy at the orchard most

days. Speaking of… "I didn't know that Robbie Bradford was back in town."

"Oh." Cora didn't blink at all now. Her blue eyes were as wide as they were in their mother's favorite baby picture of Cora, taken her first Christmas when the tree lit up the front bay window. "Oh, you didn't know?"

Britt gave her a wry look. "Of course I didn't know. You didn't tell me." They talked at least once a month, after all.

"Well, it never came up. I thought that maybe Amelia did. Or Dad…" She bit her lip nervously.

"Nope, no one told me. Not even when they asked me to help out at the orchard. Everyone still failed to mention that Robbie was not only back in town, but employed at the family business!" Her heart was hammering at the mere idea of it. Robbie! At her family's orchard. He had some nerve.

"We know that you don't like talking about him," Cora said gently. With a grin of pure relief, she looked over Britt's shoulder. "Oh, there's Amelia now!"

It was just as well, Britt thought. There was no use getting herself worked up over any of this, not when her father was inside, injured, in pain, and in need.

Guilt brought tears to her eyes as she greeted her sister Amelia, who she knew had done the job she couldn't: taken care of the house, the family, and their father all those years. She'd never complained. But Britt wasn't oblivious to how hard that must have been.

"Are you sure you and Maddie can get away from the café for the night?" Britt asked. It was a Friday night in June, meaning the place would be flooded with tourists.

"Don't go putting your management consultant advice on me," Amelia said, grinning. "I have staff, and I'm entitled to one night off. This reminds me of those Sunday night dinners we used to have, remember?"

A lump built in Britt's throat, and she managed a nod.

"Besides," Amelia continued. "It's not every day that my big sister is back in town."

Big sister. It had been a long time since she'd heard that, even if she didn't exactly feel like she'd earned the title.

"Have you seen Dad yet?" Amelia asked, and Britt shook her head. "And Cora told you about the caregiver?" She flicked a glance at Cora, who stayed quiet.

"Thanks for arranging that," Britt said to her sister. She sighed deeply as she turned back to the porch steps. "I suppose we'd better go in."

Maddie's bike was already propped up on the grass—it was the same one she'd had as a teenager. She led the way, her sisters seeming to mutter to each other as they followed her, up the stairs to the front red door where a cheerful wreath was hung on its center, probably from Cora's shop, judging from the boxwood. She felt the strange need to knock, but knew that was silly because this was her home; her bedroom was just up the stairs, between Amelia and Cora and across the hall from Maddie. With its view of the lake stretching out before her, it had been her favorite place in the world once.

Of course, they had all moved on. Cora now lived above her shop and Amelia had a small house in town, where she rented out the first floor to Maddie, for what

Britt knew was a steep discount. It was just her father here now, in this big house that seemed to have a life all of its own at times, when they were all together inside it, singing carols at Christmas, or putting on Sunday night plays or made-up dance routines for their parents, or running out the back door to the waterfront on the first warm day of the year.

The last time she'd been inside this house, they'd all still been tucked in their rooms, their dolls on the shelves. It had been a sad house then that she was leaving. One filled with loss, as much as it felt empty. But now it had a wreath on the door and the windows were cracked for fresh air and her sisters were smiling and happy.

She wondered how she looked to them. If she looked equally happy. Because in her heart of hearts, she wasn't. She was just as empty and lost as she'd been fourteen years ago when she thought leaving here was the only hope she had.

She didn't know what she expected when she walked through the door. Dread, heartache, the reminder that the house was empty, that her mother was no longer in the kitchen, nowhere at all. She assumed her father would be upstairs, in bed, propped up on pillows, perhaps asleep with the aid of painkillers.

Instead, she saw her father sitting in the front living room, on his favorite chair, a tray at his side, and a woman—a woman who was most definitely not her mother—holding his hand.

Her expression must have betrayed her shock because the woman immediately smiled, patted his hand, and rose. "Why, this must be Britt!"

Her hair was…big. Blond. Not a natural shade, either. And her blue eyes were eager as she blinked rapidly, approaching Britt faster than she could back up.

Her father turned to get a better look, but before Britt could greet him, she was squeezed against the rather robust bosom of this strange woman who wore entirely too much perfume.

"I'm Candace," the woman said when she finally released her. "But everyone calls me Candy because I'm so sweet." She giggled at her own joke. And snorted. And in addition to too much perfume, she also wore far too much eye makeup for this time of day, Britt thought.

Or maybe she was just being unkind. Because this woman was not her mother. And this woman should not be in her house. And she most definitely should not be holding her father's hand.

She darted a glance at Cora and Amelia, who seemed to gulp. "This is the caregiver we told you about," Amelia said, a little breathlessly. Cora was frozen at her side.

Britt felt her shoulders relax a bit. Well, in that case…

Now *Candy* had linked arms with her and was leading her deeper into the living room, where her father was happily munching on a bowl of mixed nuts, a glass of something that most definitely wasn't water within reach on the television tray.

"Hey, Dad," she said. Awkwardly, she unhooked herself from Candy and reached down to hug her father, blinking back the confusion as she searched his face. His grey eyes were bright and downright merry, and his cheeks were full of color. He was the picture of health, aside from the cast on his leg and on his arm, of course. And if she didn't know better, she might almost say he seemed…happy.

And not just because she was home.

"What have you got there?" She motioned to the amber-colored liquid in his glass.

"Candy poured me a glass of cider." He looked past her to give Candy a rather familiar smile.

Britt glanced over her shoulder at Candy, who beamed back at Dennis and then turned her attention back to her father. "Hard cider?"

"You know it's how I like it," he replied, and then laughed when she frowned. Deeply.

"Oh, I know everything you like, Denny," Candy said with a little giggle.

Denny?

Behind her, Britt thought she heard one of her sisters snort, but she was too frozen to react, to give them the death stare they deserved.

Instead, she narrowed her gaze on her father. "Is that a good idea, Dad?"

He brushed a hand through the air, barely disguising his amusement. "Aw, loosen up, Britt. In the old days, they medicated people with stuff like this."

"It's the twenty-first century," Britt said pertly. Then, because she couldn't resist, she slid a glance at Candy and said, "And you have medical help tending to you."

Tending to more than his broken bones, she was starting to think.

"Oh, now, I'm not a nurse in the medical sense," Candy corrected, giving her a little wink. She arranged the pillow behind Dennis's back and said, "But I do know how to make this man feel a little better. Don't I, Denny?"

To her horror, her father winked up at Candy and whispered in a husky voice, "You certainly do, Candy."

"I'm worried, Dad," Britt blurted before she could even process a polite reaction to this situation. Really, this was just all too much. Candy had to be a good ten years younger than her father. He was a weak man! He had broken two bones! Her heart was racing as she considered how to resolve this problem. "The orchard is fine. I stopped by on the way here. I think it's better if I focus on taking care of you. The business can survive a few weeks without you."

Especially with Robbie on staff, she thought bitterly.

"Oh, now, don't you worry your pretty little head," Candy said, giving her shoulders an affectionate squeeze. "You just leave your father's care to me. Besides, he told me you had a brilliant mind for business."

Britt felt her shoulders sink with shame. Brilliant enough to be cut in the first round of layoffs. She knew it was business, and that she suggested staff cuts all the time when she evaluated other companies, but she couldn't help but wonder what she'd done wrong.

"He told you that?" she asked, weakly.

Candy grinned. "Oh, he's told me *everything* about you."

Britt looked wryly at the woman with the unnaturally blond hair that hung in bouncy curls at her shoulders, and down to the scoop-neck blouse, that revealed other potentially unnatural assets, and then slid her father a glance, pursing her lips at the boyish grin on his face.

"I'll go say hello to Maddie," she said, forcing a smile as she turned, only then allowing a look of wrath to fall on Cora and Amelia, who were all but cowering in the corner, wringing their hands.

They followed her quickly, seemingly as eager to get away from whatever that was as she was, and didn't speak again until they were in the kitchen, where Maddie was standing at the stove top, her brown hair pulled into a loose bun, just like the way their mother used to style her hair.

Maddie turned, giving her a shy smile, and Britt felt another pang. Of all her sisters, Britt spoke to Maddie the least. She'd only been thirteen when Britt had left home, just a little girl really, who used to follow Britt around and ask her to braid her hair.

And at Brooke's wedding, she'd still seemed young, still eager to share her news with Britt, still wanting to hear her advice.

But now...

"You're all grown up," Britt said, a little wistfully.

"We've all grown up," Maddie pointed out, her mouth pinching a little as she motioned to Britt's outfit. Gone were the cut-off shorts and tank tops. She was sensible now. Crisp, white linen pants that made for easy travel. A sensible cotton top that stopped at her elbows.

Britt waited, but Maddie made no show of coming forward with a hug, and Britt could only stand there in confusion. Was Maddie mad at her about something? Wasn't she happy to have her back?

"I assume you've met the nurse?" Maddie asked as she opened the oven door and checked on something, before resetting the timer.

Britt's mouth thinned as she glanced at Amelia and Cora. "Is that what you guys are calling her?"

"He's a lonely man," Cora urged, and Britt softened. Slightly. Since their mother had died, their father had never dated, never even expressed a desire to do so. He'd busied himself at work, and raising his girls. Aunt Miriam had helped out, of course, but for the most part, Dennis was on his own.

"I never thought that he might be lonely," Britt said, saddened at the thought of it.

"Let him have a little fun," Maddie said, turning back to the stove top, and Britt was surprised to realize that her baby sister was giving her advice for once. "It will be over soon enough, once he's back on his feet."

"He's happy, and he really does need the extra set of hands," Amelia urged, and then, after a brief hesitation, she added, "I mean, someone has to help him in and out of the shower."

Britt blinked at her sister as the entire room fell silent, and then, at once, they all burst into laughter.

*

The conversation stayed on safe topics (the upcoming Cherry Festival which was considered Conway Farms' biggest event of the year, the weather, business at Amelia's café, and Uncle Steve's upcoming vacation) until the plates were cleared.

By Candy. Who seemed to have made herself right at home.

"That was delicious, Amelia," Britt said, meeting her sister's eye.

"Oh, this isn't from the café," Amelia said nervously. "Candy made tonight's dinner."

Did she now? Britt was suddenly angry at herself for clearing her plate, and not just because of the calorie consumption. Everyone knew that mac and cheese was her favorite meal as a kid, but she wasn't a young girl anymore, or even a teenager. But somehow, in this house, she was frozen in time.

"Maddie helped while I was busy tending to Denny, of course. But I wanted to do something special for all of you girls for making me feel so at home," Candy said with a smile. "And when your father mentioned to me that macaroni and cheese was your favorite, Britt, I simply couldn't resist."

"That was very thoughtful of you," Britt managed. She met Cora's eye, who gave her a pleading look, the same look their mother had once given when they were still at that age of feeling the need to bicker over trivial things like who had the biggest slice of cake and who got more marshmallows in their hot cocoa. The look said *be nice*, and Britt was nice.

But she didn't like having things sprung on her. First Robbie. And now, Candy.

"I made dessert," Maddie said, disappearing into the kitchen.

From the open door at the end of the dining room, Britt could hear Candy and Maddie chatting while dishes clanked and drawers were opened. She sighed, thinking of Cora's words. Their father was a lonely man. It hurt her heart to think that he had been so strong for all of them, that she hadn't even picked up on the fact that he was still suffering too.

She turned to him now and reached out for his hand that was poking out of his arm cast. "I missed you, Dad."

"I missed you too, sweetheart," he said, his eyes kind and so familiar, that Britt felt a lump rise in her throat. "I can't thank you enough for taking time away to come help out like this. I know how busy you are with your big job."

She released his hand and folded and unfolded her napkin. "It's not a big job," she huffed. It was no job at all, in fact. She took a sip of her water to settle her nerves.

"Big enough to keep you too busy to visit more often," a voice cut in, and Britt looked up to see Maddie giving her a hard look.

Candy stood in the doorway beside her, wagging her finger in Britt's direction as if she were a child who had just tried to get an early taste of dessert. She smoothed over any confusion with a big smile. "Your father talks all about you girls. I swear, this past week, I feel like I've come to know you as my own."

Cora cleared her throat. Amelia lowered her eyes.

Britt pulled in a calming breath as Maddie set a pie in the center of the table. A pie that looked exactly like the ones that their mother used to make for them, every Sunday night for dinner. Most were sold at the market, but she always kept one tucked away, just for the family.

Britt felt her eyes well and forced herself to think of other things.

"So, um, Candace—"

"Candy. Please." Again a giggle. Again a snort.

Britt swallowed hard, and, with all her willpower, managed to say, "Candy. Do you have any children of your own?"

"I haven't been blessed in that department," Candy said as she slid back into her seat on the opposite side of Dennis. She gave him a suggestive smile. "Yet."

Britt met Amelia's eyes across the table and she knew from the look in them that she was dangerously close to one of those giggling fits she would get as a child at the most inappropriate times, like when Maddie had accidentally burped at Grandpa's funeral. But she'd only been four then. It was excusable.

Britt watched her go through all the emotions, the internal struggle, the will to fight through it, to not even question the most obvious matter. Just how old was Candy?

From the looks of her, she was right around fifty. In other words: too young for Dad.

And wrong. All wrong. But then, was anyone right? He was their father. Their mother's husband. Their wedding photo still hung on the gallery wall going up the stairs. They had been the perfect couple.

"Modern medicine is a wonderful thing, isn't it?" Candy was saying now, and before Britt could even respond, Amelia was muttering something under her breath as her chair squeaked against the floorboards, and then she was gone, through the door, leaving the rest of them hanging.

Maddie quickly cut the pie, handing out plates to everyone who held their hand out. Britt looked down at hers with a heavy heart. If she stayed like that, she could almost believe that when she looked up, she might see her mother sitting across from her, her blonde hair coming loose from her bun in wisps, her cheeks flushed from standing in a hot kitchen for so long, making her blue eyes shine extra brightly.

Instead, she looked up and saw Candy, digging into her slice, groaning with each chew. "This pie is worth breaking my diet for," she declared, patting her curvy figure.

"Just like Mom used to make," Britt said sadly, as she picked up her fork. She hovered the tines over the crust, almost afraid to cut into it, for fear that it wouldn't taste the same, that it would be different.

Just like everything else.

But Maddie had learned from the best. Stayed by their mother's side in the kitchen for hours every weekend and after school, too.

And thank God for that, Britt thought, giving her sister a little smile, even if it wasn't returned.

Something had remained the same in this house after all. Even if everything—and everyone, it would seem—had changed.

3

Britt awoke to a noise that was foreign to her, and not because she was in her childhood, twin-size bed in Blue Harbor, rather than her more comfortable queen back in her apartment in Chicago. She blinked against the sunlight that was pouring in through the parted pink-striped curtains that framed her window, trying to place the sound. Birds didn't make that sort of call, and she didn't think her father had gotten any cats or other pets since she'd been away.

Though given everything else he had forgotten to mention, she supposed it was entirely possible.

She tossed off the floral-printed quilt and reached for her old, grey sweatshirt—with a small tear in the sleeve and threadbare in the elbows, it was the one article of clothing that she'd kept from her high school days and brought with her to Chicago, and she still took comfort in wearing it when she was hanging out at home, or in lonely hotels on her frequent business trips.

The digital alarm clock that had sat on her white bedside table for as long as she could remember flicked over to another minute. It was early, even for her, and she usually rose at six to hit the gym before showering and grabbing a coffee to go before settling into her office by eight. Or, when she was on the road, which was more often than she was in Chicago, she was the first person in the hotel exercise room or indoor swimming pool, doing laps.

Even after she'd lost her job last month, she stuck to her routine, altering it to a run along the lakefront, and a coffee and shower at home, before settling into a long day of job searching. She approached her job search as one would a job. She didn't leave her desk aside from lunch, and she applied to at least four jobs a day, even if it sometimes took all day to find four worth applying to.

But now it was so early that the sun hadn't even come up. Early enough for her to hopefully have a nice coffee with her father and catch up before she left for work—and figure out why in hell he had hired Robbie Bradford as the manager of their family business. Their history was hardly a secret. But then, nothing in Blue Harbor was, and that was half the problem.

The smell of freshly brewed coffee filled the air as she walked down the stairs. Her father had been set up in his study, and she supposed it was a blessing that many of these old homes had full bathrooms on the first floor of the house, even though they'd only ever used that particular tub to hose off after playing outside when they were kids.

Still, it was convenient now, given that her father couldn't exactly make it up and down the stairs in his condition. She was impressed he was even able to get into his wheelchair on his own, much less start the coffee, until she walked into the kitchen and saw Candy standing at the stovetop, singing.

The woman couldn't sing, but it didn't seem to stop

her. She reached for every note, dragging out the syllables as if she were holding a microphone, not a spatula. Her hair was already styled into curls that bounced at her shoulders. Eggs and bacon sizzled in the frying pan, and despite herself, Britt's stomach rumbled.

"Oh." She stopped short of the doorway to the kitchen, uncomfortable with being alone with this eccentric woman, and then quickly walked to the cabinet next to the window and reached for a mug. She busied herself with preparing a cup of coffee just the way she liked it: with a splash of fresh cream from the dairy farm at the edge of town. It beat any national coffee shop chain.

"I didn't realize you'd be here so early," she said, taking a sip. After all, Candy had still been here last night, when Britt had retired to bed shortly after her sisters had left, exhausted from the long drive, and so much to absorb in one day. Seeing Robbie. Meeting Candy. Knowing that everyone had moved on. Everyone except for her.

"I'm staying here," Candy said with a smile she threw over her shoulder. Already, her lips were painted a bright red color. "Your father needs round-the-clock care."

She turned to face Britt head-on and it was only then that Britt noticed that over her low-cut, skin-tight blue cotton shirt, Candy was wearing her mother's apron. The apron that should have been hanging from the hook, where it always hung when her mother wasn't wearing it. The apron that never should have been worn again.

That did it. Britt left the kitchen and went down the hall to the study, not sure if her father was even awake, but assuming he must be. No one could have slept through that noise.

Sure enough, she found him on the pullout couch, propped up on pillows, a glass of orange juice within reach on his good side, the *Harbor Herald* unfolded on his lap. The curtains to the wall of windows looking facing the lake had been pulled back, filling the room with light.

She scanned the room quickly, even though she wasn't sure what she was looking for exactly. Red lace lingerie? A silk robe? There was no evidence that Candy had slept in here last night. Really, she needed to calm down. And looking at her father, so content and happy, she knew that she should.

"I didn't realize that Candace was staying here," she said in what she tried to pass off as a light, chatty tone. Still, she gave him a long look. *Please, Dad, say it isn't true. Say you aren't falling for this woman. Say that you still love Mom. That you haven't moved on. That you haven't forgotten her.*

That she isn't gone.

"*Candy* is staying in the old sewing room. She didn't want to mess up any of the rooms upstairs, and she said it was better for her to stay close."

The sewing room had been her mother's little hideaway in a house that was otherwise overtaken by the four girls and their endless mess. Britt prickled at this and said, "I hope she didn't rearrange anything in there."

Her father's eyes drooped a bit. "She's gone out of her way to be considerate. She's a great woman once you give her a chance."

Britt pursed her lips, forcing a nod. "She's certainly friendly."

"Isn't she?" Dennis leaned forward eagerly, his smile

so wide that Britt decided to drop it. Even if Candy was wearing her mother's apron. And sleeping in her mother's sewing room, which wasn't so much of a sewing room at all, but more of a study space, a little nook of the house where she had a pinboard full of pie recipes tucked amongst photos of the girls at various ages. Where she used to wrap their Christmas gifts and stow them under a blanket, long after they'd all stopped believing in Santa.

She walked over to her father's desk and dropped down onto his leather swivel chair. She'd spent many afternoons in this room as a child, doing her homework at the big wooden desk, far away from the commotion from the rest of the house, but close enough to still feel a part of it.

She picked up the framed photo of her parents on their honeymoon and studied it, even though she had it memorized by now. Now, though, she was amazed by how young her parents looked in the photo. Younger than she was now. Their entire lives were spread out before them. None of this—this house, her sisters or her—was part of their lives then. All they had was each other. And the orchard.

She set the photo back with a frown, noticing that her father's expression had sobered.

"Dad," she said, giving him a frank look. "Why didn't you tell me that you hired Robbie?"

"I knew this was coming," Dennis said with a sigh. He folded his paper as best he could with one arm, giving her his full attention. "We all know what a sore subject he was. Sore enough to keep you away all those years."

That wasn't why she'd stayed away, not really, but somehow it didn't feel fair of her to tell her father that the real reason she stayed away was because it hurt too much to come back. That it wasn't home anymore without her mother.

That she wasn't as strong as all of them were.

That being here hurt almost as much as it hurt to stay away.

"I didn't know he was back in town."

"Well, now, he came back about a year ago, after his wife passed," Dennis said, and Britt felt her composure slip.

She knew, of course, that he had gotten married. It had slipped out the one time she'd visited for Brooke's wedding, when her father had consumed a little too much wine at the table and the talk was all about weddings, of course. Her sisters knew better and had danced upon the subject, waiting for Britt to bring it up, and she'd heard Amelia reprimanding him out on the dance floor later that evening when they thought she couldn't hear.

Married with a baby, that was the last she knew. Living in Boston. Beyond that, she had chosen to exist in a bubble, hadn't even gone on social media. Had confirmed her belief that it was best to put Blue Harbor, and her past, behind her for good.

Only now Robbie was back. And he was single.

"I had no idea," she said. Her mouth was dry as she tried to process this information.

"He doesn't talk about it much," Dennis said gruffly. "But I can sympathize with the man. Raising that little girl

on his own. It isn't easy, and he needed the work, not just for the money, but to keep busy. He has a strong business background. And he knows the business. He practically grew up in those fields."

That he had. Right at her side.

"Well, when you put it like that, I don't suppose there's much I can say," she said a little reluctantly.

"Besides," Dennis said. "I thought you were dating someone."

Dating was a stretch. A big one. Every now and then a coworker set her up, but nothing that ever seemed to stick. Nothing that she particularly wanted to stick, perhaps. She was better on her own, focused on her career, bouncing from city to city, and dropping back to her home base in Chicago for about a week out of every month.

Except now she had no career. And the last few weeks she had spent in her apartment had made her realize just how little she had invested into it. It was temporary, in many ways. Like everything else.

There was a rustling at the open doorway, and Candy appeared with two plates of steaming food. "Knock, knock!" she said cheerfully, using her hip to push the door open wider. She'd removed the apron, at least, only now she revealed skin-tight leggings in a bright turquoise that left very little to the imagination. "I hope you have an appetite this morning, Denny! Made you your favorite. Bacon, eggs, and Candy's famous cheese biscuits." She laughed loudly and gave Britt a big wink.

Britt glowered at her father, but when she saw the delight in his face, she decided it was time to leave. Now wasn't the time to be lecturing him about his cholesterol. Or telling him to close his eyes as Candy bent over him, her ample chest in prime view as she set the tray on his lap.

"Well, I should go," Britt said, standing stiffly.

"I have plenty if you'd like me to fix you a plate!" Candy grinned as she tucked a napkin into the neckline of Britt's father's shirt and patted his chest in a way that could only be called unprofessional.

Britt stared in silence, wondering if she should ask for Candy's credentials, or if her sisters had bothered to check any old references, but again, her father was pink-cheeked and alert, eating a homemade breakfast that she hadn't prepared for him. Who was she to talk?

"Thanks, but I think I'll have a quick shower and then stop by the café, visit with Amelia before things get too busy." She managed a tight smile, but it immediately slipped when she watched Candy pick up a fork and spoon-feed her father.

Last she had checked, his right arm was perfectly intact. But he didn't protest. And from the distracted wave he gave her as she walked toward the door, she had a bad feeling that he would be milking this injury long after she'd left Blue Harbor.

Which was exactly why he couldn't know she had no good reason to leave.

Other than Robbie Bradford being back in town.

*

A PLACE FOR US

Because the weather was so nice, and because Britt's gym membership back in Chicago was paused until she had gainful employment again, she went to the garage behind the house, hoping to find her bicycle still in working order and happy to see that it was right where she'd left it. Her sisters' bikes were gone; no doubt put to daily use. There was something to be said for living in a town small enough that you didn't always need a car to get around.

She climbed on it, wobbling only a little as she took off down the street, grinning to herself at what a simple pleasure it was to ride a bike, to feel the wind in her face, and the fresh air in her lungs. Back in the city, she took public transit everywhere, and she only even owned a car because she'd needed one for all her work travel.

Travel that made staying in a relationship difficult, not that she was looking for commitment anytime soon. If ever. After all, nothing lasted forever, even if you thought it would. Or said it would.

She arrived in town quickly and hopped off the seat so she could walk her bike the rest of the way. The sidewalks were heavy with tourists who flocked to the area on the weekend year-round, but especially in the summertime, and the numerous inns that lined Main Street all boasted a No Vacancy sign.

The Firefly Café was just off Main, right along the beachfront and not far from the harbor, where sailboats docked, and ferries came in and out to Evening Island. Amelia had just taken over the café from its former owner before Britt had been here five years ago, and she was eager to see how it had come along.

But first, she needed to have a word with her sister.

Amelia was behind the counter when Britt pushed open the blue-painted door. The room was filled and smelled of blueberries and cinnamon. On the blackboard that hung over the counter was the daily menu of various egg dishes for breakfast, and soups, salads, and gourmet sandwiches for lunch all sourced from local farms and artisans. Two younger women that Britt didn't recognize were taking orders, each wearing a blue-striped apron that coordinated with the café's logo.

Amelia was icing a tray of fresh cinnamon rolls. The smell was so good that Britt almost forgot her reason for being here, and she was starting to regret not at least grabbing a cheddar biscuit from the kitchen before she'd left home, even if Candy had made them.

"Hey you!" Amelia's cheeks were flushed and her blue eyes were bright. Her strawberry blonde hair was pulled into a tight bun that showed no signs of coming undone.

"Those look amazing," Britt blurted, as Amelia dropped another dollop of icing onto the rolls and the sugar immediately started to melt. Her sister hadn't gone to school for cooking, but she clearly knew everything she needed.

"Tell Maddie that," Amelia said, motioning to the window pass to the kitchen. "She makes me two pans of these every morning, and they sell out faster than I can finish icing them. I'm not complaining, though. The demand gets people in my door earlier than usual."

"I got the impression that she was upset with me last night," Britt confided quietly. When dinner was over,

Maddie had been the first to leave, and something told Britt that it had nothing to do with Candy's storytelling about her brief stint on her high school diving team. ("Just rolled into the water like an egg!" she'd hooted, much to Dennis's delight).

"She's just worried about Dad," Amelia said distractedly.

Maybe, Britt thought. Still, she wasn't convinced. "That pie was good. I tried to compliment her."

Amelia met her eyes and smiled. "As good as Mom's."

Britt swallowed hard.

"Is she still making pies for the market?" Once, they had always sold her mother's pies, but Maddie had taken over that responsibility as soon as she was old enough to handle the job—when their mother was too weak from her treatments to continue the task that she had loved.

"Oh, yes," Amelia said, moving the tray of cinnamon rolls to the side. She glanced at one of her helpers and sighed. "I think these will be gone before I can even cut you one."

Britt grinned. "How'd you know?"

"Because I know you. And because I doubt that you stuck around the house long enough to eat one of Candy's deep-fried meals."

Britt laughed, despite herself. "Why didn't you guys tell me she was staying at the house?"

"I assumed you knew." Amelia looked at her quizzically. "Dad can't move around on his own."

"But Cora said that you're bringing meals over to the house!"

Amelia gave her a knowing look. "Someone has to give that man some healthy food. If it were up to Candy, every meal would be comfort food." She slid a cinnamon roll across the counter and cocked an eyebrow. "Not that I have room to comment."

"She sings," Britt said.

Amelia's brow knitted briefly. "Who sings?"

"Candy. She sings while she cooks. In Mom's apron."

Amelia did her best to compose her features, but Britt could tell that she was far less offended by this than Britt was. Maybe because she hadn't been subjected to it firsthand.

"I'll bring her over one of our aprons today when I drop off lunch. Chicken salad. With fruit. If Dad won't eat it, help yourself."

"Thanks," Britt said, feeling better. Still, she'd feel better after tasting this cinnamon roll. She reached for a fork while Amelia poured her a coffee. "I'm going to need to reinstate my gym membership if I keep eating this way," she said.

"Why'd you cancel it?" Amelia asked, and Britt felt her face flare.

"Oh." She stumbled for the best excuse. Really, she could tell Amelia anything, she knew, but somehow, the thought of leaving again, when she didn't have to, made things overly complicated. Overly personal. And she didn't want to hurt her family, even if they understood her reasons for staying away. "I didn't see a point in paying for the month if I'm here for three weeks."

"Think you can survive three weeks of Candy's singing?" Amelia grinned, and Britt gave her a dark look.

"More than I can handle three weeks of Robbie Bradford," Britt said. She shoved another bite of the cinnamon roll into her mouth and sliced off another piece before she had finished chewing. Wow, this was good. "Nice warning, of course. Though I suppose if I'd known that he was back in town, I would have stayed away."

"Britt, um—"

Amelia's face flushed as low laughter filled the room. Britt stopped chewing the cinnamon roll. She gripped the fork in her hand. She knew that laugh. Knew it too well. So well that it had taken more than a few years to get the sound out of her head, and even more years to stop wishing she could hear it again.

She swiveled on her stool to see Robbie put down the newspaper that had been shielding his face, a grin spreading all the way up to his eyes.

"Glad to know you still care, Britt," he said, casually leaning back in his chair.

She stiffened. Did her best to finish chewing the roll in the most dignified manner possible, which wasn't easy, considering the piece she had shoveled in was on the large side. Very large. After much struggle, and with the horrifying awareness that Robbie was watching her the entire time with a glint in his eyes, she swallowed, feeling it move painfully slow down the length of her throat.

"Didn't your mother ever tell you it isn't polite to eavesdrop?" she finally said.

"Oh, I wasn't eavesdropping," Robbie said with an open smile. "Your sister knew I was here the entire time. Can I help it that my ears started burning?" He stood, folded the paper, and dropped a bill into the tip jar on the counter.

"Thanks for the coffee, Amelia," he said. He slanted her a glance, when she had just started to think he might leave without saying anything more to her at all. "I'll see you soon, Britt. If I haven't scared you straight out of town."

He was still laughing as he pushed out the door, and Britt turned to give her sister a glare that she had mastered a good twenty-five years back.

Amelia just gave a helpless shrug in return. "I tried to warn you."

Yes, Britt supposed she had. But it was too little too late.

For a lot of things.

4

Unless it was picking season, the orchard's operations were closed on the weekends, but Sunday, rain, snow, or sun, the market was open for business, and Britt arrived early to help out—and escape Candy's morning serenade.

After leaving the café, hot with embarrassment, she'd spent most of yesterday in the quiet solitude of her father's office, a cup of coffee on the desk, going over her father's books and getting reacquainted with the business. From her job as a management consultant, she liked to take the time to familiarize herself with a business on her own, before getting employees involved, and any chance she had to distance herself from Robbie, the better. From what she'd reviewed so far, she had some concerns about the business's longevity, but one thing was clear from the invoices she'd looked over, and that was that Maddie's pies were a big seller at the market, just as their mother's had been. Back then, people used to line up outside the barn doors, hoping that they had arrived early enough to snag a pie before they were sold out. For many in town, this was the dessert for their Sunday night dinners. It was a treat they looked forward to after a long, hard week, and Britt's mother prided herself on the fact that she was able to bring a little cheer to everyone's household.

She suspected that Maddie's reasons for continuing the tradition were slightly different, but one thing was clear, and that was that people in town couldn't get enough of these pies.

Britt managed to slip down the stairs early Sunday morning unnoticed. Candy was crooning too loudly in the kitchen to hear the front door open and close, and Britt rode away on her bike with a sense of relief. The orchard was only a couple miles outside of the center of town and she arrived quickly, happy to see that the market wasn't scheduled to open for another twenty minutes, which should give her plenty of time to talk to her sister and glean some insight into the weekly event.

Maddie was already setting up at a table near the front door with a few of the full-time staff when Britt walked into the converted space. The entire barn had been transformed into a store years ago when their grandfather had first bought the land. Back then, they were only selling fruit locally, but even after the sons took over, and their cider and wines were sold in local businesses and spread to surrounding townships, the market remained open on Sundays to support the community of Blue Harbor, though sometimes Britt suspected that her father only did it because Britt's mother loved selling her pies there so much.

Over the years, the market had grown. There were ciders and juices and jams and pies and baskets of fresh fruits and berries. In the fall, they hosted the Harvest Fest when the grapes were ready, and in the spring, they had the Blossom Barn Dance. A few weeks from now, come early July, would be the Cherry Festival, which had been Britt's favorite as a kid—the height of summer.

Today, Maddie was selling strawberry pie. She had at least a dozen white boxes stacked in front of her, and Britt knew from her cursory research that, much like the cinnamon rolls she made for Amelia's café, they'd be gone all too soon.

"Good morning, Maddie!" she said cheerfully. She was met with a tight smile in return, confirming her suspicions that something was definitely up with her youngest sister. She tried again, saying, "You must be busy, working at the café, and making all these pies."

Maddie shrugged away the compliment, saying, "It's not a big deal. And I enjoy it."

Britt frowned at her, wondering where the hurt came from in Maddie's eyes, and if she had somehow put it there. It had been months, she now realized, since she had spoken to Maddie or even texted with her. She'd felt caught up on all of Maddie's news through Amelia and her father, but now she realized that this might not have been enough.

"Maybe we could meet for a drink one night this week," she offered, but Maddie just shook her head.

"Summer in the Square is next weekend and I'll be working overtime at the café to help Amelia prepare. She's enlisting all of our help on Saturday, by the way."

Britt hadn't even thought of the festival in years, even though it once used to be a highlight of her childhood. Stores opened their doors and held a sidewalk sale, and on Saturday night, there was a big event on the lawn, with food stands, live music from local bands, and games for the children.

Right now, the thought of facing the entire town of Blue Harbor in one sitting felt like too much, but if it gave her a chance to spend time with her sisters, she'd take it.

"Count me in," she said, and judging from the raise of Maddie's eyebrows, she was beginning to question if she even had a choice.

"I hear these are a big seller," Britt tried again, motioning to the pies.

"Well, it's a good recipe." Maddie struggled to meet her eye as she rearranged some pie boxes.

Britt fell silent as she gave her sister a sad smile. "It's the best."

Maddie nodded. "She was the best."

There was no arguing with that. And no replacing her either.

Britt thought about what her father had said about Robbie's wife and wondered if he felt the same. If, like her father, he would stay single, never date, never open his heart again.

It didn't matter, she told herself. Just like it didn't matter that Robbie was back in town. What they had was ancient history, and clearly, it meant nothing at all. He was her high school boyfriend, and the last thing she needed to worry about right now when she still had a job to find and her father to worry about—and not just because of his two broken limbs.

Still, her heart tugged a little when she looked over and

saw Robbie walk through the open door, looking just as handsome as he had back when they were teenagers, his wavy brown hair slipping over his forehead in a boyish way that made her stomach flip, despite knowing better.

She patted her hair and straightened her blouse just the same. Looking her professional best, she told herself.

"What's he doing here?" she grumbled to Maddie as she watched Robbie clasp hands with some of the locals who were already gathered at the doorway.

Her sister just shrugged. "He's the manager. He comes every Sunday."

Britt thinned her lips. He may be the manager, but she was family. And technically, her father had put her in charge of the business in his absence.

"I've got things covered today," she said lightly as Robbie approached, wearing jeans and a light blue plaid button-down shirt that was rolled at the sleeves. She was starting to regret her decision to wear light grey slacks and a silk shell top because from the way he was looking her up and down, he wasn't checking her out.

"I didn't realize we'd gone corporate," he observed.

Britt gave another self-conscious pat to the tight bun at the nape of her neck and said, "Just professional. This is a business, after all, even if it is a Sunday."

Maddie muttered something about needing to check the stock of the jams and slipped away, leaving Britt to deal with Robbie on her own.

"It's a *local* business. And the market is a community event," Robbie countered.

Britt lifted her chin a notch, refusing to defend herself.

"Still, there are no reasons to let standards slip. This is my *family* business, and my father did ask me to oversee things."

"Temporarily," Robbie said pointedly. He raised an eyebrow. "You do know you're wearing silk in a barn right now."

"I didn't realize you knew your fabrics so well," she replied steadily. "Besides, this is a store. A *converted* barn." She gestured to the gleaming exposed beams, the polished hardwood floors they stood on, and the bright white walls that boasted large, colorful framed oil paintings that a local artist had done of the orchard years back. Each wall shared a different season. Winter had always been Britt's favorite because it was so quiet and serene.

Robbie's mouth quirked, but he just lifted his eyebrows. "If you say so. Boss."

Her nostrils flared. "I'm not your boss." She was his…nothing. She was nothing to him. He'd made that clear. And he was nothing to her. Just a painful reminder of the past. Like she needed another one.

"Good." He set his hands on his hips. "So you don't need to send me away. It's my job to be here on Sunday mornings, and I don't intend to go anywhere."

"Neither do I," she said.

"Well, that's news to me," Robbie said. "Last I heard you couldn't wait to get out of this town."

"My home is in Chicago now," she said, even though she wasn't so sure about that. Since graduating from college, half the time she was living out of suitcases in extended-stay hotels as much as she was in her apartment, which bore bare-bones furnishing and take-out containers instead of groceries in the fridge. Traveling so much for work didn't leave much time for friends, much less relationships, and other than her neighbor across the hall, an unmarried and childless woman in her late sixties who liked to make pleasant small talk when they bumped into each other outside their doors, she really didn't have much to return to at all.

But she didn't have much reason to stay, either.

"Chicago isn't that far from here," Robbie said, and Britt opened her mouth to defend herself before deciding against it. She was here to work, not argue, and besides, Robbie was correct. Chicago was over half a day's drive from Blue Harbor. It wasn't the distance that was keeping her away.

And he knew it.

Britt glared at him, but even though the words hurt, she knew there was truth to them.

"I visit. I've visited," she snapped. "And I call. All the time. I know everything that's going on around here."

He lifted an eyebrow.

After all, her father had failed to mention that Robbie was back in town and had been for more than a year. Or that his wife had died, three months before that. Or that he was now the manager of the business.

Robbie held up his hands. "I'm not here to judge."

"We both left town, Robbie," Britt said with a sigh. "We both made our choices a long time ago."

"And now we're both back, and we'd better learn to work together, at least temporarily," Robbie said. He gave her a long look. "It's what your father wanted."

Britt narrowed her eyes on that statement. It was what her father wanted, she realized, and why was that, exactly? Her father knew how hurt she had been by Robbie. That he'd chosen to attend college locally when he could have come away with her.

When he'd let her go, and didn't even try to stop her.

And when he'd moved somewhere else, after saying he would never leave. He'd moved on. Without her.

"Your father is thrilled to have you here," Robbie added.

"And how do you know that?" she asked, as she smiled at the stream of people now entering the open door, grabbing baskets on their way.

"Because he talks about you all the time," Robbie said mildly.

Britt didn't know how to reply to that. She frowned, wondering just how close her father and Robbie were, and what Robbie knew about her life. Did he know that she was single, woefully so, and that the only consistent men in her life in the past few years were named Ben and Jerry?

"Britt!"

Britt turned away from Robbie to see her cousin Gabby striding toward her, her arms full of sunflowers. As usual, Gabby looked beautiful, with glossy auburn hair and a smile that always lit up her eyes. She'd been in Britt's grade growing up, and no matter how close they were, Britt couldn't help but feel sometimes that she was living in her cousin's shadow.

She embraced her with a big hug, the flowers pressing

against Britt's back, before pulling back to dart her eyes over at Robbie. "Hey, Robbie."

"Hey, Gabby." He gave her a friendly smile and something twisted in Britt's gut. Something that could not be jealousy. That would be ridiculous! Gabby was her cousin. Her beautiful, sweet, and yes, single cousin.

Who lived in Blue Harbor. Like Robbie. Who was also single.

She blinked hard at the stems in her cousin's hands and forced her attention back to business matters. Comfortable terrain.

"Do you sell these here?" They'd never sold flowers at the market before, but then, as Robbie had pointed out, she hadn't been to a Sunday market day in as many years as she'd been gone.

"Just some seasonal bouquets," Gabby explained as she walked over to the table beside the pies and set them down. "I have more to get out of the back of my car. It was my dad's idea, and Robbie agreed."

Britt gave him a sidelong glance. Did he now?

"I'll let you ladies catch up," Robbie said, backing away. "I should really tend to the guests and make sure everything is in working order, anyway."

Britt opened her mouth to protest. Shouldn't she be the one to greet everyone at her family's market? But he had a point. He'd been working here for over a year now, and the last time she'd helped out, she'd been a teenager.

A teenager very much in love with the man who now turned and walked away from her.

For the second time in her life.

*

Robbie climbed in his truck and flicked on the radio. One of his favorite songs was playing, but it did little to lift his mood. Frustrated, he switched it off and focused on the road ahead.

Keira was spending the day with his parents, who had promised to take her to the beach for the day with their neighbor's granddaughter. Robbie was all too happy to give Keira the chance to build a friendship and have a little fun, and he had intended to use this time to catch up on work, try to come up with a strategy for paying off that business loan before Britt got her hands in things and had room to comment. Present a case to Dennis Conway upon his return, because the man was set in his ways. And in the past.

Not that Robbie supposed he had room to talk.

Now, with Britt hanging around the orchard, questioning everything from the price of the jams to the cost of the labels, he saw no use in sticking around unless he wanted to end up in an argument with her before dusk.

And from the way things were going, he had a bad feeling that the argument could turn personal. And there was no room for personal feelings when it came to Britt Conway, and not because she was his boss's daughter, either.

He pulled up to the Carriage House Inn, knowing that his older brother, Jackson, would be inside, managing the pub that pulled in as many locals as it did visitors. The inn was one of several in town, each similar in appearance with their white paint and black shutters and quaint fur-

nishings inside. The competition was friendly because tourists flocked to Blue Harbor from spring through fall. The Winter Carnival at Christmastime was nearly as big of an attraction as the summer festivals and the lure of the scenic lake views and cool, clear water. There was something quiet and charming about the town when the snow fell. It was an escape. From the hustle of daily life.

Or from memories of the past.

Only with Britt back in town, it seemed that some of that past had encroached on his present.

He bypassed the lobby door and instead took the side entrance, directly into the pub which was open to patrons as well as the public. It was a dark room, with scuffed walnut floorboards and black Windsor chairs. The menu options trended toward comfort food, and Robbie's stomach grumbled as he slid up to the bar, where his brother was polishing wine glasses.

"What can I get you? Cider? Beer?"

Robbie glanced at his watch. It was early afternoon and already the day felt long. "Coffee. And...the burger."

"Meaning cider and the cheeseburger, extra fries." Jackson grinned.

Robbie shook his head. "I don't have the same freedoms as you," he said. "I'm picking Keira up in a few hours and I'm watching my cholesterol."

Jackson's expression sobered, and Robbie almost wished he hadn't brought it up. Jackson knew the reasons why Robbie wanted to stay fit, and it wasn't because he was trying to attract the ladies. Far from it. He had a daughter to protect, and he wanted to be there to raise her. And Stephanie's cancer diagnosis had hit him out of nowhere. She was the healthiest person he knew, taking a daily jog, maintaining a vegetarian diet, and even popping a multi-vitamin each morning with her green tea. If she could get sick, what hope was there for him? And where would that leave Keira? He was all she had left.

"Coffee coming right up," Jackson said, slinging a towel over his shoulder. He put the order slip into the kitchen and returned with a steaming mug. "So when were you going to tell me that Britt Conway was back in town?"

Robbie looked up at him. "You knew?"

"I hear everything in this place." Jackson grinned. "But it's Blue Harbor. *Everyone* knows everything. And the Conways are a big family around here."

That they were, with Dennis's four daughters and Steve's three. Seven pretty girls. Seven single girls. At least, he assumed Britt was single. Dennis had never mentioned a boyfriend. Sometimes, Robbie wished he wouldn't bring her up so much, but then he thought about Keira, his heartwarming at the mere image of her, and he knew that Dennis was just a proud father. Certainly, there wasn't any more to it than that.

"Everyone was wondering what would happen when Dennis took that fall," Jackson continued. He helped himself to a cider, ignoring Robbie's look of passing judgment. "As you said, little brother, I have my freedoms."

That he did. Unmarried. Unattached. No kids. He was two years older than Robbie, but when it came to life experience, Robbie was ahead. More ahead than he'd planned, he thought, his mind once again trailing back to Stephanie.

"There are some perks to settling down you know," Robbie advised him, but Jackson just shook his head. Keira had been the greatest gift from the moment he first held her in his arms, bundled in a striped cotton hospital blanket.

He had no idea then just how much he would need her.

"Why would I want to settle down when I'm perfectly fine on my own?" Jackson's grin was wicked. "While you're grocery shopping and meal planning, I'm playing pool down at Harrison's Pub. And when you're filling in camp forms, I'm down at the water, sitting on my boat with a cold one in my hand and the wind in my hair."

Robbie raised his eyebrows and took a sip of his coffee. He wasn't sure why he would encourage his brother to pursue a relationship when he had no plans for one himself.

"You've always been the one who seeks out relationships," Jackson continued.

"Not anymore." Robbie stiffened his back. He didn't appreciate the cock of his brother's eyebrow.

"Think she's back for good?" Jackson asked and stepped back to lean against the counter. He wasn't going to let the topic of Britt drop.

Robbie shook his head. "Just until Dennis gets the arm cast off." Luckily, it was just a fracture and didn't require more extensive measures.

"You okay with that?" Jackson asked, and Robbie gave him a hard look.

"Of course," he said, only from the heaviness that landed squarely in his chest, he wasn't so sure that was true at all.

But Jackson didn't seem to have any interest in jabbing him on the topic anymore today. He jutted his chin, looking at something over Robbie's shoulder as his mouth curved into a grin. "Well, look at that."

Robbie didn't like the sounds of this. "Look at what?" he asked, refusing to turn around and see what—or whom—his brother was talking about.

Jackson's eyes gleamed as he set down the cider and tapped the space next to Robbie's coffee mug a few times. "Like I said. Small town. Bound to hear things. Bound to run into people."

With a grin, he pulled the towel off his shoulder and walked around the bar toward the back table near the window, where Gabby Conway was just taking a seat, across from Britt.

Robbie swore to himself under his breath and wondered if it was too late to cancel that burger. Or too obvious to take it to go.

Jackson, meanwhile, for a man who claimed he had no interest in a relationship, seemed to have no problems chatting up the ladies with the ease of a professional. And that was exactly what he'd call it if Robbie questioned him, Robbie knew all too well. Professional hazard. Part of the job. He was friendly. He was in the business of keeping his customers happy. Especially ones of the female (and attractive) persuasions.

If Britt had seen him, she didn't react. Her back was to him, her hair still pulled back in a no-nonsense knot. She was still wearing that ridiculous, stuffy outfit. She looked like a different person. And she was a different person.

The girl he used to know was gone. And she'd left a long time ago, long before he'd stopped waiting for her.

His brother caught his eye, and, not much different than he used to do back when they were teenagers and Jackson was up to trouble and thought that Robbie was a little too stiff for his liking, he decided to stir things up, and held his hand, drawing attention to the man at the bar with his coffee, just trying to mind his own business. Just trying to do his thing.

Just trying to get through each day since his world fell apart fifteen months ago.

Jerk. But he couldn't stay mad at Jackson. Never could. His brother, like his parents, was one of the reasons he'd moved back to Blue Harbor. Sure, his excuse was that Keira needed family, but the truth of it was that he did, too.

He might be a single dad. And he might stay that way. But he couldn't be completely alone.

Britt looked over her shoulder with curiosity, her annoyance showing the moment their eyes locked. She turned back to Gabby immediately. Jackson watched it all with an amused grin. He claimed the best part of the job was the daily drama that unfolded. Didn't even need those television sets hanging above the bar.

Right. Forget the burger. Robbie didn't need it anyway. He should head home. Get some things cleaned up before Keira returned. Make sure he got her registered for camp before all the spots filled up, now that Jackson had reminded him about those darn forms. Summer break was just around the corner.

Keira would come home soon. They could take a bike ride. Clean up the yard and plant those flowers he'd been meaning to get around to. Put down roots. Maybe they'd order a pizza. And then she'd go to bed.

And that was when things got tough.

He slapped some bills down on the counter and, heaving a sigh, finished the last of his coffee and pushed off his stool.

His brother looked at him in surprise as he patted him on the shoulder. "Heading out?"

"I have to get some stuff done before Keira gets home," he explained, knowing that Jackson would never argue with anything when it came to his niece.

Robbie glanced at the table. Gabby's face was friendly, in an open smile. Britt, however, was giving him an icy stare.

He tipped his chin. "Ladies. There's a burger on the way to the table if you'd like to share it."

"Thanks!" Gabby exclaimed.

Britt's shoulders relaxed a bit at this, and she gave a reluctant smile.

"You didn't have to," she protested.

"It was that or let this guy eat it," Robbie said good-naturedly, but it hurt him, bantering like this, almost as much it hurt him to argue.

Once, he and Britt had been close. Closer than he was

to Jackson. Closer than he'd been to his wife in many ways.

Now, they were strangers. It felt tense. And unnatural. And wrong.

And for reasons he couldn't describe, it felt lonely.

5

Britt was sitting in her father's office, a spreadsheet open on the computer screen before her, open files of invoices and bank statements spread out on the desk. The coffee in her mug was cold when she reached for it, and that was the second time that this had happened this morning, since she'd arrived early, wanting to get a start on things before Robbie came into work.

Now, she knew she couldn't wait any longer for some caffeine. And the dull headache that was starting to rear probably had more to do with her withdrawal than the numbers she'd been staring at for hours.

She went down the hall to the staff kitchen, a small room with just a mini-fridge, sink, and enough counter space for the coffee machine, hesitating in the doorway when she saw Robbie filling his mug. She glanced at her own, wondering if it was really worth it, but considering the orchard was on the edge of town and she couldn't exactly just walk around the block and find the nearest coffee chain, she supposed that it was.

"Hello," she said, walking into the room.

He looked over at her with mild surprise, his eyes roaming over her body with the sole purpose she knew of judging her choice of attire. She pushed back the twinge of disappointment that Robbie seemed completely disinterested in her appearance, much less attracted to her when she couldn't help noticing that time had improved his looks. His curly brown hair was cut shorter now, and he had a five-o'clock shadow on his strong jaw. His shoulders had filled out from his boyish frame, and he stood taller, with more confidence, like he belonged here. And maybe he did.

She pushed her pride to the side as she dumped her cold coffee down the sink and filled it again. "So as manager," she started, leaning against the counter as she took a sip of her coffee. Oh, that was good. About as good as the patient expression that Robbie was giving her. Robbie. Her Robbie, standing just a few feet away from her in jeans and a button-down shirt, and brown leather boots that were much more practical than the patent leather stilettos she was wearing. Or the pencil skirt that did seem unappreciated in this casual environment.

"What is it exactly that you do?" she asked, genuinely curious about his daily responsibilities and how they could be made more efficient.

He seemed to bristle at this, emitting a look that told her he didn't appreciate being called into question. But finally, he replied, "I oversee all the crops. I oversee the Sunday market. And I oversee all the events that take place at the orchard."

She nodded. "Like the Cherry Festival."

"And the Harvest Fest. And group tours or school events," he said. "We have one this afternoon."

"And how much do we charge for the school to come through?"

He gave her a long look—long enough to tell her the answer.

"What about wine tastings? And I don't mean a sampling in the market on Sunday. I mean a real proper tasting, with pairings and a farm table in the vineyard. That kind of thing would be perfect for a girls' weekend—"

Robbie shook his head. "That's all Dennis. He oversees the distribution and business end of things. I run the daily operations."

"But you're not a farmer," she said to him, trying to see if he could explain this to her.

"No, but I spent half my childhood on this orchard," he said frankly. No room for nostalgia there. "And I paid attention."

"And so did I," she said, pushing away from the counter. She glanced toward the door to see if anyone else was nearby, but the building that housed the business offices had always been limited to two offices, a small meeting room, and this kitchen. They were alone. And she suspected he was just as aware—and just as uncomfortable with this—as she was.

Still, she hesitated before eventually speaking her mind. "Did you know my father had to take out a loan last year?"

Robbie didn't look surprised by this. "We had a bad apple crop last fall. Too much rain will do that, but you know that." He shrugged. "Without apples, no cider. No picking activity, either. Without cider, no sales. Sure, we made do, but the numbers were down. There was no avoiding that."

She shook her head. "The problem is bigger than that. Selling things locally, even regionally, well, there's only so far you can take it."

He narrowed his eyes at her. "What are you saying?"

"I'm saying that we have a good product here. Our ciders and our wines could really sell if we had better distribution."

Robbie shook his head, chuckling softly. Britt frowned at him.

"What's so funny?"

"You," he said. "Coming in here, trying to make things bigger and better. You've been here since when? Friday? Afternoon? Your father's been doing this for his entire life. Some years are going to be better than others. I'm fully aware that the numbers don't look good. I've seen enough to know that times are tight. You can't control Mother Nature."

There was something in his eyes that told her he knew there was more to this than too much rainfall.

"No, but you can have a bigger profit margin to offset a bad year."

"And what do you propose exactly?"

"Progress," she said evenly. "And growth. Has anyone considered expanding the product line, offering more than cider and wine?"

"Cider and wine are what Conway Orchard is known for. It's our brand."

She bristled at the possessive tone he had taken but decided not to comment.

"And it's not enough," she said impatiently. She

huffed out a breath and leaned a hip against the counter as she met his eye. "You can't move forward without growth."

"Growth? Or change?" he asked, frowning deeply at her.

"Aren't they one and the same?" she replied evenly.

"And aren't you leaving in less than three weeks?" he asked pointedly, and she knew he had her there.

Even if she didn't technically have to go anywhere. But with her father back at work, there would be no room for her here. And, from the look of things, no way of paying her either.

"I've been known to turn around entire companies in less time than that, or at least give them a plan to get them back on their feet."

He picked up his mug and walked to the door. "Maybe so, but we aren't a company, we're a family business. Your family business, as you keep pointing out. But I don't think your father wants you coming in here and trying to fix things."

She held up a hand. "I can deal with my father."

He shrugged. "I'm just saying that I've worked with the man for over a year now. This isn't about growing the business to him. It's about protecting a family legacy. He's proud of the traditions he has in place here, and I'm grateful to be a part of it. So there was a bad year. I'm fully aware."

"I'm trying to help. And I think I know my father a little better than you do, Robbie."

He raised an eyebrow, silencing her, and a terrible shame twisted her stomach.

"If you want to help, then I suggest pitching in on everything we need to do to get the Cherry Festival going. We have less than four weeks now and I'm sure your dad will want to return to work knowing that everything is ready."

She nodded. He had a point there.

But that still didn't mean she would stop there. The Cherry Festival wasn't just their biggest day of the year. It was also the perfect time to test new products and see what they could do to move Conway Orchard out of the past.

And maybe, to bring her out of it too.

*

Britt finally looked up from the stack of paperwork in front of her just as a bright yellow school bus pulled into the public lot near the barn. Even through the warm breeze filtering through her open window, she could hear the small, excited voices of the children as they were led through the berry path, buckets in hand, by Dory Williams, the woman her father had employed to give tours long before Britt had even been born.

She smiled, thinking of how huge and exciting it had felt as a child to roam through the rows of trees and bushes, to pick a treat right off a branch, and taste a strawberry or cherry when it was warm and ripe.

The sun was shining and the sky was blue, not a cloud in it. She had a pair of sandals in the trunk of her car. On a whim, she decided to put them on, take a walk through the fields and see all that this school tour entailed and if anything had changed over the years—though, knowing Dory's enthusiasm for sharing all her knowledge and all her stories, Britt could only assume that much had stayed the same.

Like pretty much everything around here.

Still, some fresh air would be nice, and she hadn't said a proper hello to Dory, who spent all her time outside, while Britt remained inside. Maybe she could poll the kids for a few ideas for improving the place. Do a little due diligence while she was at it, without Robbie making observations or shaking his head.

She frowned to herself as she walked to the car and swapped her heels for the much more comfortable flats. A business couldn't just stay the same, year after year, and expect to thrive. Even her father had recognized this when he'd taken over the orchard and started making wine.

She'd talk to him, soon. If she could ever get a word with him away from Candy.

Her lip curled on the image of Candy spoon-feeding her father a bowl of chocolate chip ice cream last night. She didn't know which part was worse, that her sixty-year-old father with a fully functioning right arm was being spoon-fed, or that Candy knew that his favorite flavor of ice cream was chocolate chip.

Or that there was a woman living in her house who was not her mother.

She slammed the trunk of her car a little harder than necessary and turned back to the fields. The kids were up ahead, in the cherry orchard, learning all about the growing process from Dory, who never spared a detail, no matter how tedious. She was an older woman now, a little frailer than Britt remembered, but the energy of the kids seemed to bring out her smile.

And she'd always been proud of these cherries. No doubt, any chance to show off a bit of her effort was enough to brighten her entire day.

Britt glanced at a few as she walked over to the group. Not ripe yet, but it wouldn't be long now...

And the Cherry Festival was a huge draw for tourists. Robbie was right; if she put her energy into making it a huge success, then they could make up their losses from last fall and maybe even pay off that loan before it came due in a few short months.

"Hello!" A little girl with dark hair and big brown eyes stopped walking with the group and waited for her. "Are you here to pick strawberries too?"

Britt considered this. It hadn't been part of the plan, but seeing the hopeful expression on the child's face, she wasn't exactly sure how she could resist.

"I don't have a basket," she said with regret. It would take too long to turn back now.

"You can share with me," the girl said happily.

Britt felt a sense of warmth spread over her that she hadn't experienced in a workday—make that any day—in...well, a long time. Too long, she thought, as she maneuvered her pencil skirt to crouch beside the girl. Too much of her time was spent in boardrooms, in suits, meeting with people whom she would leave and never see again, floating from one concrete building to the next, one hotel bed to the next, never making anything, or anyone, permanent.

Never getting too close.

"Oh, not that one," she said gently, guiding the child's hand away from a cluster of berries that still needed at least another week to grow.

"Oh, I know!" the child said proudly. "You don't pick the green ones. You pick the red ones. I know all about which berries are the best."

"Is that so?" Britt looked down, amused, as she dropped a few strawberries into the basket that sat between them. "Did Dory tell you?"

The little girl shook her head. "My daddy. He knows all about these things. Basically, he knows everything."

Britt grinned. She used to think that about her father too. Still did, in many ways, even if his judgment was clearly off, and not just about the state of the business's finances. Her mouth pinched when she thought of the way his eyes watched Candy as she fluttered about, trying to look useful. Trying to look something, that much was for sure.

Feeling connected to the little girl, she leaned in, glanced around, and said in a stage whisper, "You know, the best way to tell if a berry is ready is to taste it."

She popped one into her mouth, smiling at the taste, and, after a moment, the little girl did the same, giggling the entire time.

"I think those are pretty perfect," Britt said. They tasted the same now as they had when she was just as small as this girl, and if she closed her eyes, she could almost believe she was still that young again, carefree and full of hope before everything changed.

"Sampling the product, I see," a voice boomed behind them, and Britt shot up, even though she knew it was silly. This was her land. Her family's property. But somehow, being away, she no longer felt like she held a place here.

Before she could rise to her defense, the little girl shot past her, squealing, "Daddy!" before launching herself at his chest, her arms tight around his waist.

Britt stared at Robbie, trying to read the look in his eyes. He was wary, maybe even concerned, and he was looking at her for an explanation.

"I didn't know this was your daughter," she clarified. She grinned at the little girl, now noticing for the first time what must have drawn her to her in the first place. The same brown hair as Robbie. The same warm, chocolate eyes.

She pulled in a breath. This was Robbie's child. She'd known she existed but never saw pictures. Once, there was a time when she imagined her own children with Robbie, but here they were, so many years later, and despite all their dreams and plans, they hadn't happened.

Not for her anyway.

She took in father and daughter for one more aching second and then held out her hand, "I'm Britt Conway."

"Like the name of the farm?" the child asked, reaching out to take her hand. "I'm Keira."

"Britt's my boss," Robbie told Keira, and then glanced back at Britt, his look challenging but slightly amused.

She sighed, grinning a little. "Not really. Your dad and I are...old friends."

That was one way of putting it, she thought. More like first loves. And in her case, only loves. She pushed aside the hurt in her chest as she met Robbie's gaze. Did he still feel it? The connection? The memories? The attraction? Judging from his demeanor, he felt nothing at all.

But then, he'd moved on a long time ago, hadn't he? While she...she'd simply moved away.

"You know my dad?" Keira's face lit up.

Britt nodded. "That's right. We used to play on this very farm. In fact, your dad used to help me pick all these strawberries so that my mother could make jam."

"I like jam," Keira said, grinning. "Does she still make it?"

Britt felt her smile slip. She swallowed back the lump that made it hard to speak, to even breathe. This was why it was easier in Chicago, or on the road, where people didn't know her past and didn't really ask much about it, either. Where no one had to know that she'd lost her mother when she was only eighteen years old. When she didn't have to miss her so much or think about her every day.

"No, she...she passed away."

"Oh." Keira's expression immediately fell. "My mommy's in heaven too."

Britt looked up and met Robbie's gaze. His eyes were flat, his jaw set, and he silently reached down and took his daughter's hand.

Britt remembered what her father had said, about giving him this job, about knowing how he felt.

Robbie was raising this little girl all on his own. Now, seeing them together, she couldn't help but think of her own father, and how he must have felt, with four girls under his roof, and then three when she left.

Was it any wonder he'd never dated? There was no time.

But Robbie... She didn't allow that thought to bloom.

"What else did you and my daddy do?" the girl asked.

Britt caught the mirth in Robbie's gaze and did her best to keep a smile from forming, but there it was all the same. She didn't allow herself to think of the past—the good times, or the bad—but now, with Keira staring at her expectantly, she saw no choice.

"Well, we used to go swimming. And ride bikes." Britt paused as a memory came back to her. "And once your daddy and I had a contest to see who could pick more strawberries, and I couldn't understand why the more I picked, the less I had in my basket."

Robbie was watching her carefully, as if he too had forgotten that day until now.

"Did he take them?" Keira looked at her father, aghast.

Now Britt grinned. "Turned out he was eating them."

Robbie laughed, a sound that was loud and rich and achingly familiar, even if she hadn't heard it in nearly half a lifetime.

"It was payback," Robbie chimed in. "Britt and I were always trying to outdo each other. Once, Britt dared me to see who could climb higher on the big maple tree in front of her house. And guess who got stuck on a branch with no way down?"

Britt narrowed her eyes at him, but she couldn't push away her smile. "My father would have eventually gotten me down," she said.

"Or the fire department," Robbie pointed out.

Instead, it had been Robbie who climbed up on his own and guided her back down the tree until they were on firm ground. Hand in hand. Arm in arm. He'd kissed her then, their first kiss. Right up against the trunk of that old tree. She hadn't even cared if her sisters were watching out the window, and they had been, of course, they had. They'd heard her screams when she couldn't get down from the top branch and Robbie had made a big show of saying he had somewhere to be, have a nice night…

She swallowed hard, pushing away the memory of his kiss. The sweetness of it. The way it had taken her by surprise yet felt so natural all at once.

"You know," she said, leaning down to give the little girl a smile. "I bet that if you fill that basket with strawberries, you could have enough to make a strawberry smoothie for breakfast tomorrow."

Keira squinted up at her and shook her head. "I'm not sure my dad could handle that."

Britt burst out laughing, and even Robbie joined in. "Oh, I bet he could," she said, giving him a rueful look. "He's pretty amazing, your dad, you know."

She locked eyes with him across the little girl's head, and for the first time since coming back to Blue Harbor, she didn't feel the need to run from the memories of the past. For just this moment, she was happy to have them at all.

6

Every Thursday after school, Keira went to an art class in town, and Robbie's fridge was now covered in her weekly creations, ranging from watercolors to pastels to some three-dimensional creations he'd had to ask her to explain to him, lest he call it something it wasn't, like the time he thought her clay sculpture of a polar bear was a cat. The weekly activities were something he'd put in place as soon as he'd returned to town. Structure. Routine. Keeping busy was better for both of them, and it wasn't much fun for Keira to spend every afternoon hanging out at the inn with his mother. So there was ballet and art class, and in the summer there would be camp. Last summer had been the most difficult, of course, with Keira wanting to be by his side, not used to being sent away for the day since Stephanie had worked part-time from a home office.

Now, a year after they'd returned to Blue Harbor, he couldn't help but reflect on how far they had come. He didn't have the same sense of apprehension when he sent her off to school in the morning or went to pick her up at the end of the day. As he climbed out of the truck and walked up the gravel path to the doors of the cottage that served as one of several local art studios, he felt comfortable and even relaxed, and at home.

As difficult as it was to start over again as a single father, coming back to Blue Harbor had been the right choice. It was home. It always had been. And Britt had reminded him of that today. There was history here. Laughter. Good times. Times that he didn't think about often enough, because so often it was easier to forge ahead, without looking back.

Inside the studio, parents were busy collecting their kids. It was a small space, with a large table in the center of the room, and trays of supplies in the center to share. Today's project had involved painting birdhouses, and Keira excitedly held up her messy creation.

"Can we hang it up on the tree in front of our house?" she asked hopefully.

Another reason to come back here, he thought, as he admired her handiwork. Back in Boston, they had lived in a condo in a high-rise building that overlooked more buildings. They didn't even have a balcony; the only thing Keira knew of nature was from their trips to the park and playground. Here, they had a house, a yard, trees, and fresh air. Keira was thriving, which Robbie knew would please Stephanie, even if it did make him feel guilty for having this daily joy that she had been deprived of, her life cut unfairly short.

He knew it was his responsibility to give their daughter the best life he could, but it felt wrong to see her adjusting, and moving on when he couldn't bring himself to do that.

He still yearned to talk to Stephanie or turn to her when things became too overwhelming, like when Keira

got the stomach bug or the time she lost her favorite stuffed animal, and Robbie didn't even know which one she was talking about, because they all looked pretty much the same and had similar names too, all cutesy, many named after some sort of color or food group. He had mistakenly assumed that Rainbow was the pink unicorn and Coco was the brown horse, but it turned out that Coco was the brown bear and Rainbow was…Well, he didn't really know what Rainbow was, at least not for a while. Now he knew. She was a lama. And a unicorn. How that all worked, he didn't know, but there it was all the same. It had taken over a year of doing this on his own to learn the ropes and to be a family of two instead of a family of three.

But they'd done it. They'd made it.

"She has quite a unique style." The art teacher, a woman a few years younger than him, who had long, flowing red hair and bright blue eyes, set a hand on his arm and looked at him so earnestly that he had to glance away.

There really weren't enough single men in this town, and that was the problem. He'd love to offer up his brother, but seeing as Jackson was hell-bent on staying single, he doubted that this would be much help. Besides, Mila was pretty, and this town was small. Jackson had probably already dated her, considered dating her, or was still considering dating her. And with dating Jackson came inevitable heartbreak. At least with Robbie, there was no chance of that. For anyone.

He carefully stepped back, retracting his arm. "She

gets it from her mother," he said, honestly. Stephanie had been a costume designer for several local theatres, and she was always sketching something, or admiring different colors, getting new ideas. She had made many of Keira's clothes when she was little. Now, they were all too small. Figuring out what size clothing to buy Keira had been another learning curve. One they'd figured out. Together.

He glanced at his daughter now as she came and took his hand. Gone were the mixed prints that she, then at the age of five, had to instruct him did not match. He had chuckled, thinking of how much she had learned from her mother, but his heart had felt like it was splitting in two when he hoped that she would hold onto it, that this wisdom would last her a lifetime, because it had to.

Now Keira was dressed in a pink cotton dress and functional slip-on sneakers in sparkly canvas. Her hair was pulled back in an albeit messy ponytail, but he could at least say she had started the day with it looking neater than the just-rolled-out-of-bed look she had going for a while there. Had it taken about a month to master that ponytail? Yes. Could he do the braids she was asking for? Not yet. But he was watching online videos. He'd get there soon.

The art teacher gave a little sigh and moved on to another parent who had just come through the doors, giving Robbie the opportunity to slip out without any more exchange.

He breathed in the cool, early evening air, something he had never appreciated until he'd gone without it, something he hadn't even missed until he'd rediscovered it.

Time had a funny way of doing that.

With people too, he thought, as his mind drifted back to Britt.

"Can we order a pizza tonight?" Keira asked as they loaded up into the truck, and he made sure her seatbelt was secure.

He laughed. "No, we cannot have pizza tonight. That's for weekends."

True, it used to be a daily thing, in the beginning, because cooking had never been his strength either, and because ordering takeout was just so much easier. But there weren't many options for that sort of thing in Blue Harbor—another adjustment.

"I'm grilling chicken for us tonight," he said. "But if you want, we can swing by the store on our way home and pick up something for dessert."

"Brownies?" Keira asked with a devilish look.

He gave a rueful smile. "I was thinking ice cream."

She loved to push, and once he would have caved, but that was the easy path, and this parenting thing…it wasn't easy at all. Especially on his own.

But bringing in another person wouldn't make things any easier, he told himself every time things got difficult or the nights felt lonely. It would only complicate things. For him. And for Keira. And he couldn't afford to let that happen, not when he now had not just one, but two women leave his life without warning.

Even if one had returned.

*

Britt had decided that enough was enough. She'd been in town for nearly a week, and in that time, it seemed that Candy was determined to feed her father a steady diet of so-called comfort food. It was time to get some fresh produce in the house and make herself more useful. Besides, Amelia had her hands full at the café; there was no reason for her to be troubling herself with dropping off meals that Britt knew Candy usually just set aside and never served, even if Britt did enjoy them for herself.

She stopped by the grocery store on her way home, happy to get a space just in front and knowing that it wouldn't be this easy come tomorrow when tourists flocked to town for a summer weekend. She could only hope they would also flock to the market on Sunday. Now that it was deep into June and the weather was warming up, it was the orchard's best time to recapture some of their losses during the other less busy seasons.

She laughed at herself as she pushed through the door into the air-conditioned store. Maybe Robbie was right. She was only here temporarily, and she couldn't stop looking at ways to improve things. She couldn't help it; it was in her nature. Righting wrongs, turning bad situations into good ones, and breathing life into dying companies had kept her going since she had graduated from college. It wasn't just the escape. The travel and the moving from place to place had been the distraction she needed, sure. But she thrived on the ability to take something that felt hopeless and salvage it. To know that some things were still within her control.

She might technically be unemployed right now, but

that didn't mean she could sit back and relax. When you relaxed, things fell apart. And helping the business was the only way she could help her father.

Or herself.

She took a cart and began pushing it through the aisles. Even though she hadn't been back to this store since she'd come here as a kid, with her mother, she remembered the layout, with the fresh items around the perimeter and the processed and frozen items distributed through the six short aisles in the middle. Small, but efficient. She saw no room for improvement here, and she liked to think she had a trained eye.

In no time, she had collected enough to at least get her through the weekend, and, with any luck, offer up a meal or two to her father (and Candy, she thought, with a sigh) that might offset all the cholesterol that Candy was feeding him.

She unloaded her items and scanned her card. And waited.

"I'm sorry." The teenage boy behind the counter gave her a nervous glance. "It said the card was declined."

"Really?" Britt froze, but her mind was on overdrive. She had paid off last month's statement, at least the minimum balance, and her next payment wasn't due for another two weeks. She surely couldn't have already exceeded her limit—could she?

Her heart began to pound as her cheeks turned hot. She'd been cash poor recently and knowing that not much would be coming in had made her rely on credit more than usual. But she hadn't kept track. And now…

"I'll try again," the boy offered, even though she wished that he wouldn't. A line was starting to form and she could feel the heat of several pairs of eyes on her. "Sometimes there's a glitch with the system."

Britt managed a watery smile, but she was starting to shake. She should leave, collect her maxed-out credit card and what was left of her dignity, and go to the car. She'd call the company when she got back to the house. Transfer some funds out of her savings account. Only there wasn't much left in there anymore. Rent in Chicago was steep. And she hadn't received any more responses to the jobs she'd applied to, or any feedback from the interview last week.

With a heavy heart, she knew she could always tap into her special savings account where she had a small but not insignificant inheritance from her mother. She'd held onto it all this time, hoping she would know how to use it, and when.

Sure enough, the kid shook his head. "Nope. Declined again."

Really, did he have to say it quite so loudly? She narrowed her eyes on him as she took back her card and stuffed it with a shaking hand into her wallet.

"If you have another form of payment—"

"You know, I'll just come back for these," she managed. Her face was burning, and she kept her eyes low, unwilling to look around her and take in all the curious gazes.

"You sure?"

He just wasn't going to let this drop, was he?

"I'll take care of it," a voice behind her said.

Britt closed her eyes against the shame because as much as she wished the husky, deep voice belonged to her father or her uncle, she knew that it of course belonged to Robbie.

He was standing beside her now, giving her a grin so wicked that she managed to forget her humiliation for a moment as a mixture of fury and gratitude spread over her.

"Just combine it with my items," he told the kid behind the counter.

The kid shrugged and began scanning the new groceries before Britt had a chance to protest. "Thank you," she managed, but her voice was locked in her throat and she still couldn't bring herself to fully look at him.

They were standing close, so close that she could feel the rise and fall of his breathing, sense the hair on his arm against her own bare skin, and she moved to the side, waiting for the heat to leave her.

"Did she run out of money, Daddy?" a worried voice asked as Keira emerged from behind his back.

Britt gave Robbie a withering glance. He winked in response.

Ah, so this was fun for him, was it? Saving the day? Stepping in and acting all responsible when she so clearly wasn't?

"She's just having a problem with her credit card, honey," Robbie replied, giving Keira's shoulder a squeeze.

"Good thing you're here to save the day!" Keira smiled broadly and Britt managed to grit her teeth into some semblance of a smile in return.

She could feel a dull headache coming on as she waited for her bags to finish being packed. It seemed to take an extremely long time. Long enough for Robbie to calmly pay the tab. Long enough for him to saunter close to her and say, "Seems I have a knack for getting you out of trouble."

Except something told her he wouldn't be kissing her after today's rescue mission.

"I just forgot to pay the bill," she said in a huff. "I left Chicago in a rush, after all."

Technically, four days after she'd heard the news, and Robbie was no doubt aware of this. She was all too aware that her cheeks were on fire.

But Robbie just cocked an eyebrow and fought off a grin. "Must be the case. After all, you've got that big, fancy job, telling people what to do, how to run their businesses, who to keep, who to fire…A job like that pays pretty well."

She reached out and grabbed the handles of her paper grocery bags. "It does. And I should go home right now and remedy this. I'll pay you back in the morning." She stared at him, pushing out a breath. "And thank you."

"Just a little favor between friends," he said mildly. "After all, you would have done the same for me."

He had her there. It was true, she would have. But friends? They weren't friends. Friends knew your ups and downs and kept tabs on your daily life. They were there for you when you needed them the most.

Robbie was not a friend. Britt didn't have friends. Not anymore.

"Still, you didn't have to step in," she said. She couldn't quite bring herself to say the words, *help me*.

Robbie picked up his own two bags and followed her out of the store. "If I hadn't, someone else would have. That's what's nice about a small community like this. We all look out for each other."

"All know each other's business, is more like it," she said ruefully. How many times, that last year she was here, did she feel drained and overwhelmed by the endless questions she was met with everywhere she went? She couldn't find an escape, couldn't go to the library or even to a store without someone asking about her mother. She couldn't breathe in this town.

"They just care," Robbie said gently.

"It's true," Keira offered. "Natalie always offers to bring me home from ballet class and she keeps saying she can bring dinner over, too." She shot a look at Britt. "I think she knows Daddy is just learning to cook…"

Britt laughed, but the little girl's comment wasn't lost on her. She'd grown up with Natalie Clark and her sisters—spent holidays with their family when Aunt Miriam wanted to include her sister's family too. There was always a spot at the dining room table for everyone, always enough food, too. Britt's mother had made sure of that. And, looking back, she loved the house when it was loudest and most full.

But Natalie wasn't just being friendly. Natalie was a single mother living in a small town with limited bachelors. Of course, she'd take an interest in one of the Bradford boys. Who wouldn't?

Pushing aside the flutter of jealousy that had no business existing, Britt jutted her chin at Robbie as Keira climbed into his truck. "It seems that you have some admirers in town."

So a woman wanted to hint her way into a date with Robbie. Who was Britt to care? But she did, she realized. She still cared.

"There's only one girl for me," he said, shaking his head. "And she's six."

She frowned a little. "Oh. So, you haven't...dated at all?"

"Nope, and don't intend to." He loaded his bags into the back of the vehicle and met her eye.

Well, then, she thought, as she loaded her own bags into the car and waved good-bye, she supposed that took any possibility of a second chance for them off the table.

Not that she'd been planning on one.

*

By the time Britt returned to the house, she had a plan. It was what she did best, what kept her grounded and the anxiety at bay. She would spend the entire evening applying to new jobs, expanding her search beyond Chicago to the greater Midwest region. She would create a budget. And she would call her landlord to ask about breaking her lease or subletting it come July. She lived in a trendy part of the city where there was always a demand for rental space. She could do with less space for the time being; after all, she was used to living out of hotel rooms most of the time anyway.

Or…But no. Her stomach tightened as soon as the thought took hold. She could stay here, she supposed, just until something else came along. But staying here with an end in sight and staying indefinitely were two very different things, and once her father was back at work, she wouldn't really be needed much.

Still, she could make herself useful while she was here, and she intended to do that. Tonight. Before she got a start on her career plans.

She unloaded the groceries directly through the back door and into the kitchen, relieved to see that Amelia had followed up on her word and that a blue and white striped apron from her café now hung on the hook in the pantry where their mother's had always been. Still, somehow seeing her mother's apron removed, gone from its rightful place, cut her deep, and she moved quickly to focus on the task at hand. To unload all the groceries. That Robbie had paid for.

She pursed her lips as she unpacked everything. From the closed door to her father's study, she could hear the sounds of a game show on the television. Deciding to let her father be for now, and rather certain that he wasn't alone, she went upstairs to text her landlord and power up her laptop. The internet was slow, and while she waited for it to connect, she opened her desk drawers in search of a pad of paper and a pen.

She smiled a little at the contents of the top drawer. Her favorite pink eraser growing up, a single flower-shaped earring, the other long forgotten, and a few postcards that her cousin Gabby had sent her from a family vacation when they were only thirteen. And a photo of her and Robbie, taken in one of those photo booths, the strip of images black and white and small.

She remembered that day. It had been a school dance, the last one that they had gone to together, the spring of their senior year. She'd worn a pink dress and Amelia had helped her pull her hair back in a way they'd seen in a magazine. She'd gone into her parents' bedroom to give her mother a twirl, her throat closing up when she saw how pale her mother looked, how the tears that shone in her eyes seemed laced with something more than pride, and she'd suddenly lost all desire to go to the dance at all, even though she'd been looking forward to it. She wanted to stay home, in that bed with her mother. She wanted to never leave, and she only had because her mother had urged her to go out, have fun. To live her life.

Britt stared at the photo for a few minutes, seeing now that her smile didn't quite meet her eyes, that there was a shadow lingering, a reminder that she was torn, she was where she was supposed to be, but it wasn't where she'd wanted to be.

And now, now she didn't know where she was supposed to be. Or where she wanted to be, either.

Well, no use thinking about the past. She shut the drawer with a bang and held her fingers over the keyboard. She'd vowed not to dwell on those days a long time ago, and the sooner she had a new job lined up and a reason to leave this town, the better it would be to put it all behind her again.

Britt was at her father's desk the next morning when a knock at the open door interrupted her from thinking too much about the text from her landlord that had just popped up on her screen. The one that said that subletting her apartment wasn't necessary, because her lease was up at the end of the month, and while he had her, would she be renewing?

Could she even renew? She'd again wrestled with the thought of her small nest egg. Her life in Chicago. Was that how she wanted to use the funds? Anxiety squeezed her stomach and she was happy for a distraction from her problems, even if the person standing in her doorway was none other than Robbie.

"You have a minute?" he asked.

"I'm happy you stopped by, actually," she said, smiling, but the pinch of his brow made her regret her words. Quickly, she reached into her handbag and pulled out an envelope. She extended it to him. "For last night," she said.

A look of realization came over his face and he held up a hand. "No need to repay me, Britt."

There was most certainly need, and her pride was only part of it. She didn't like feeling indebted to Robbie.

Didn't like feeling that he'd done her a favor, or that she owed him. Didn't like entertaining any thoughts that they were still connected, that they still did things for each other. Even as friends.

"Please," she said. "Spend it on Keira." She grinned at the thought of the little girl.

He approached her desk but didn't take the envelope. "How about we just use it to help pay for the repair to the juicer?"

Britt felt the color drain from her face when she saw the bemused expression in his eyes and knew that he wasn't joking. "Is that what you came in here to talk about?"

"Well, I wasn't here to talk about the weather," he remarked.

Or memory lane, she thought, pushing back a swell of disappointment.

She clicked the top of her pen and set it down on the desk. "How bad is it?"

Robbie held up his hands with a shrug. "Let's just say the thing should have been replaced years ago. Last time it broke—"

She held up a hand to stop him. "*Last* time?" She knew that the commercial equipment they held in the adjacent building needed servicing from time to time, but from the way Robbie made it sound, there was a bigger problem at play.

"Like I said, the thing should have been replaced years ago."

"And why wasn't it?" It seemed like an obvious question, and one with an equally obvious answer. Money. If her father wasn't willing to replace a key piece of equipment that cost a few thousand dollars, then he must know the business was in trouble. She shook her head. "Never mind. Just show me the damage." She pushed back from her desk and stood, noticing the way Robbie's eyes dropped over her black A-line skirt and pale pink blouse. Yes, she was wearing a strand of pearls. Was it really such a big deal to dress like a professional? She was an adult woman, in her early thirties, not the young girl she'd been last time he'd seen her.

He led the way across the gravel to the next building, waving to Otis and Wally, who were labeling wine bottles, eventually stopping in the juicing room where the large, stainless-steel machine sat quiet and idle. She knew there was no sense in trying to push any buttons, but she couldn't help but be sure it was actually plugged into an outlet. No such luck.

"Now what?" She was all too aware that she was turning to him for an answer, for insight, and expertise, because even though this was her family's business, he was the one who'd been here, when she wasn't, just like he'd been quick to point out the other day.

"The repairman can be here Monday. Problem is, if we don't get these strawberries juiced, they won't keep over the weekend, or at least, they won't taste as fresh, and we're supposed to get an order of strawberry cider out by early next week." He gave her a little shrug. "Looks like we'll be doing this the old-fashioned way."

She blinked at him, wondering if he meant what she

thought he did. Back at home, and when she was younger and helping out in the business, they used small devices, meant to work in small batches, in a home kitchen.

It was something she hadn't thought about in years, something she hadn't even remembered. But Robbie had.

"I didn't even know we still had these things," she said as he pulled two small juicers from a cabinet.

"The machine isn't exactly reliable."

"And running a company without commercial-sized equipment is not the way to stay in business!"

Robbie just shook his head. "It was this way at one point in time. It's what makes Conway ciders taste so good, right? That homemade flavor? It's tradition."

She shook her head. "It's archaic."

He said nothing more as he handed her an apron from a hook on the wall and began rolling up his sleeves.

"Are we really going to do this?" she asked, laughing nervously as she tied the apron strings at her lower back.

"Unless you have a better idea?" He pulled a carton of strawberries from where they were stacked on the counter and rolled them into the colander in the sink for a rinse.

She watched the muscles in his arms strain against the weight and felt a pulling in her stomach until she had to look away.

A better idea than working side by side with Robbie for the remainder of the afternoon? She sadly couldn't think of a better idea at all.

*

They worked in companionable silence for the first

half hour, each focused on the task at hand, each knowing what to do without needing to instruct the other. Back in middle school, when it had been one of Britt's chores to tend to this task, she'd enlisted Robbie, then just her pal, to help her on days that they wanted to spend time together, and he'd never complained. Said he was just happy to be by her side.

She gave a little smile as she pressed more juice into the pitcher. She supposed she should have known then that he loved her.

Once.

"What's that look for?" he asked, giving her a sidelong glance.

She pulled in a breath, looked back down at her hands. It was easier than looking him in the eye, and the last thing she needed to do was break another machine, however small, and however familiar she was with it. Sometimes it was that kind of comfort level that led to destruction. Made you put your guard down. Made you slip. Made you careless.

Had she been careless with Robbie? Had she pushed him away? Or had she clung to him too much, when she needed to know that the person she cared most about in this world other than her parents and her sisters was a constant, steady force. That he would always be there.

Until he wasn't. He'd stood by her side, he'd wiped her tears, and he'd made her laugh, shown her how life could still go on.

But he hadn't come with her to Chicago. Said he wanted to stay. That she should too.

And then, he'd left without her.

"I was just remembering the times that we used to do this together," she said, monitoring the machine carefully. Anything was easier than looking at Robbie right now.

"You loved it," Robbie said. "But then, you loved everything about this place. You had big plans to take it over one day."

She blinked, startled that he would remember such a thing, shocked that she had forgotten it. It was true that she had loved this orchard, loved the business of it, the endless tasks that kept it running. She had loved waiting for the apples to grow and then watching them be pressed into cider. Her father had always let her take the first sip. It was their little secret, he'd told her with a wink.

She cleared her throat and rubbed her palms over her apron skirt. "Yes, well, I had a lot of plans back then."

Robbie said nothing, just set to work on the machine. She studied him for a moment but realized that she didn't need any reminders. It came back as naturally as riding her creaky old bike had.

"Who would have known that all those afternoons spent making small batches would have come in handy all these years later?"

He was silent for a minute, and when he spoke, she could hear the sadness in his voice. "Who would have known a lot of things back then?"

She looked up at him, properly, even though his eyes were now focused on his hands, on pushing the strawberries into the juicer and emptying the pitcher into the large, plastic bin they had on the counter in front of them, which would be mixed with the apple cider that was already stored and waiting.

"I have to admit that seeing you here, at the orchard, well, I couldn't have predicted that," she said, waiting to see his reaction. "One day you were dead set on staying in town. The next, I heard you were gone. Gone for good, I thought." *Like me*, she finished to herself.

"Well, it was certainly a surprise for me, too." He gave her a wide-eyed look that made her laugh.

"Not a good one, I assume," she said, fixing her eyes on the machine before her.

He looked at her until she met his eye. "I never said that," he said quietly.

Oh boy. Her heart started racing and she could feel the heat in her cheeks, knowing that she couldn't stop the blush. She walked to the sink and washed her hands. She'd already done so, and if Robbie noticed, he didn't say anything.

"Well, we're both back now. Against all odds, I suppose," she said, when she was sure her voice wouldn't betray her.

"Life is funny like that," he said with a raise of the eyebrows. "Sometimes, I look back on those days and I wonder what I would have changed if I'd known then what I do now. If I'd known how it would all turn out."

"You think you still would have moved to Boston?" she asked.

"Without Boston, I wouldn't have met Stephanie, and I never would have Keira." He looked at her. "Guess you could say I wouldn't have changed a thing."

She blinked. She didn't know why, but she hadn't been expecting that. Robbie was content with where his life had led him, or accepting of it, at least. He had no regrets, not even for not coming with her to Chicago all those years ago. Whereas she...she didn't know where her life was going anymore, and being here, next to her first love, her only love, she wasn't sure that she ever knew.

"I'm sorry," she said, glancing away. "About your wife."

"It wasn't easy at first, but we're managing," he said stiffly, returning to the juicing. "And being back in town helps, you know? There's a sense of community. It's...well, it's not as lonely here as it was back in the city."

"I kind of like the solitude of city life," she mused. "No one knows you unless you let them in." Unlike here, where she was pretty sure that Patsy over at the women's clothing boutique knew the exact bra size of every female in this town.

Robbie shrugged. "I always liked it here, but I didn't appreciate it fully until I had time away from it. Now, being back, well, it feels like I never left."

"I wish I could say the same," Britt said, reaching for another carton of berries. There was a long pause, and she knew that he was giving her space, waiting for her to fill it when she was ready. "My dad has a new girlfriend, you know."

At this, Robbie let out a whoop of surprise, and despite herself, Britt grinned. It was rather shocking, after all.

"After all this time? Who is it?" Robbie stared at her, waiting for more details.

Britt curled her lip. "His caretaker. Candace." She held up a finger, catching her error. "Correction. She prefers to go by the name *Candy*. Claims it's because she's so sweet."

Now Robbie laughed, low and steady, like a roll of thunder. "Well, I'll be. The man falls off a ladder and ends up falling in love."

Britt felt her skin prickle. "Oh, now I don't know about *love*. But...he does seem happy. Happier than he's been in a long time. Since—" She shook her head. She couldn't bring herself to say it.

"Well, good for him," Robbie said firmly.

"Yeah," she said a little weakly. "Good for him. I want him to be happy. It's just not easy seeing him happy with someone else."

Understanding clouded Robbie's gaze, and he nodded once. "I understand. It's probably one of the reasons your dad never really pursued a relationship."

"Is that the reason you aren't?"

"I've got my hands full raising Keira," Robbie clarified. "And your father had you four. Four." He let out a low whistle. "I can't even imagine."

Maddie had been thirteen when their mother died, and Cora was only fourteen, being only a year and a half different in age. Amelia had stayed most practical, getting things done, keeping busy, not showing her emotions. At the time, Britt didn't know how she did it.

But later, she learned how to do it all on her own. It was a coping mechanism. Staying focused. Staying busy.

Not letting yourself think too much about what hurt the most, not when it couldn't be changed or undone.

"He certainly never went looking for love again," Britt agreed with a sigh. She wasn't sure how she would have felt if he had. "But I guess it found him."

Robbie met her eye as they reached for the last carton of berries at the same time, their hands skimming each other, sending a shot of warmth up Britt's arm, straight to the chest. Straight to the gut.

She snatched her hand back and stepped away. Robbie looked at her, his expression unreadable, even though once she could tell everything that he was thinking with a single glance.

Or she'd thought so at least.

"I suppose that happens sometimes, doesn't it?" he said, his voice a little gruff. "Life just…happens."

Britt looked deep into his eyes, long enough to see the freckles on his nose that used to gather and build on long summer days at the lakefront, long enough to see the little scar above his right eyebrow when he'd stood a little too close as his brother had taken a swerve on the tennis court out near the old country club. Long enough to let her gaze drop to his mouth, to remember how it felt to touch his lips, to taste him. Long enough to imagine how it would feel to do that again, right here, now in this kitchen.

She cleared her throat and began fumbling with her apron strings. "It's all yours. I should probably get back up to the office anyway."

She wondered if he'd protest, or make some snarky

comment about bossing him around, but Robbie's eyes had drifted to the door behind her.

"Hey you!"

Confused, Britt turned to see Keira standing in the doorway, grinning shyly as she waited to be invited into the room.

"On Fridays, my mom drops her off on the way to her bridge club," he explained. He held up the last carton of strawberries and grinned at his daughter. "Want to help me juice this the old-fashioned way?"

"Sure!" Keira said excitedly, her eyes lighting up the way that Robbie's once did. And didn't anymore, Britt thought, with a wave of nostalgia. It was proof, she supposed, that even though they were both here, in Blue Harbor, that you couldn't go back. That they weren't the same people. Even if, for a little while there, she had dared to hope that they might be.

Robbie patiently led Keira through the steps, only after first ensuring that she had washed her hands, and of course, Keira needed an apron—it made things official.

Keira watched the juice flow through the press and grinned. "Cool! Where'd you learn to do this?"

"Britt taught me," Robbie told her. He looked up over her head and gave Britt a wink.

She felt it straight in her chest. Really, this was becoming ridiculous now.

"You must be a really smart lady," Keira said, and Britt burst out laughing.

"Well…"

"Oh, don't be humble," Robbie chided. "She is a smart lady. She has a very big job back in Chicago."

Britt felt her cheeks burn. "Well, I have a big job waiting for me next door," she said, hoping to put an end to any reference to follow her life, or lack of one, back in the city. She grinned down at the little girl. "It was very nice seeing you again, Keira."

"Are you coming to the Summer in the Square festival this weekend?" Keira asked.

Britt slanted a glance at Robbie, who was watching her expectantly.

"Please?" Keira asked, sensing her hesitation. "My painting is going to be on display and I want you to see it."

Impressed, Britt looked at Robbie, who gave her a small smile. "All the children who take art class at Mila's will have a piece on display."

Mila? The Mila who was Cora's age, with the long red hair and dazzling smile? Britt pushed back the uneasy feeling that made her heart quicken.

"And what is your piece?" Britt asked, returning her attention to the little girl. She still couldn't quite grasp how much she resembled Robbie. Those eyes, that smile.

"It's a surprise," Keira said with a giggle as a bit of juice splashed her hands.

"Even I haven't seen it," Robbie said with a shrug.

"Then I guess I have to show up, don't I?" Britt said, and Keira jumped up and down with excitement before running over to the sink to wash the juice off her hands.

"She's hard to say no to," Britt told Robbie in a low voice.

"Believe me, I know." He gave her a long look, as if he wanted to say something, but wasn't sure if he should.

"I hope it's okay," she said, wondering if he'd misread the exchange. "Amelia is enlisting all of our help anyway, so I'll be tied up at her stand for a lot of the day."

"It's your town, too," he said, lifting an eyebrow.

She considered this for a moment. She hadn't thought of Blue Harbor as her town in a long time, not since she packed her stuff into the back of her dad's car and let him drive her to Chicago. She hadn't turned around. Hadn't looked back. Nothing good came from looking back.

Still, as she left the father and daughter to juice the remaining strawberries, she couldn't resist one glance over her shoulder at the sweet moment. It could have just as easily been her standing on a chair beside her own father when he taught her how to do the very same task.

Tradition, Britt thought, as she walked outside and let her gaze fall on the rows of trees and bushes that were still here, thriving, all these years later.

Maybe there was something to be said for it, after all.

8

Maddie was already at the café when Britt arrived the next morning, wearing a yellow cotton sundress and comfortable slip-on sneakers, because she knew from past experience that there were never enough chairs or benches to go around at Summer in the Square, and from the looks of the kitchen countertops, Amelia intended to keep all of her sisters on their feet. It was a sunny day, as it tended to be on a festival day, as fortune would have it, and despite Maddie's chilly greeting, Britt was grateful for the chance to have something to do other than to worry about her unemployment status—or the fate of the orchard.

Maybe, with any luck, she would break through Maddie's shell today. Confronting her wouldn't help. She'd coax it out of her. And if that didn't work, she'd get Amelia or Cora to tell her what the heck was going on.

"Are Steve's girls coming?" Britt asked, wondering if they were enlisted to help out as well.

Amelia gave her a funny look as she stepped around the center island of the big kitchen, which felt small with every surface covered in trays and plastic containers of pasta salads. "Of course they're coming. No one misses Summer in the Square!"

No one except her was the unspoken sentiment, and Britt couldn't help but wonder if Amelia suspected that Britt would try to make up an excuse and asked for her help to make sure she would attend.

"Gabby is in charge of the centerpieces for the tables," Maddie explained. "And Jenna will be playing piano for the evening dance."

"Along with whatever high school band is playing," Amelia said with a laugh. Once, there had been a time when Amelia had a crush on the singer of one such garage band, and they'd teased her mercilessly over it.

Now, though, it seemed that much like herself, Amelia was too practical for love. And too busy, too. The café was her top priority—she'd used her inheritance to take it over, much as Cora had used her share to start a holiday shop. They'd known just how to grow what their mother had left them, whereas Britt was still struggling.

"Well, it will be good to see Jenna," Britt said cheerfully. The entire town of Blue Harbor, as well as people from neighboring towns, gathered for the annual event. Some people from Evening Island even took the ferry in for the day, and she wondered idly if her friend Naomi would stop by. They'd grown up together here on Blue Harbor, but Naomi had always pined for the island that was visible from the shoreline, and she took the ferry over every weekend she could, just for the day, to rent a bike and take a lap around the island.

"And of course Dad will be there in his wheelchair," Amelia said. The unspoken words flitted through her gaze. *With Candy.*

"Actually, I was thinking it might be too much for him," Britt said. "What if someone knocks into him? Jostles his chair?" Things could get pretty rowdy as the evening went on.

But Maddie just gave her a disapproving look and said, "You don't need to worry about these things, Britt. He's managed just fine without you for fourteen years, after all."

Ouch. Silenced, Britt stared at her youngest sister, who walked to the pantry in a huff, and then met Amelia's eyes. Amelia just shrugged and, with a glance at the clock, said, "We really need to get going."

She pushed a wisp of hair from her forehead with the back of her hand and went back to counting out the sandwiches she'd prepped in advance, and not just any sandwiches, but her famous tomato sandwiches, made on freshly baked bread that was topped with rosemary, and layered with salty artisan cheddar from a local dairy farm.

Britt's mouth watered as she stared down at the tray.

"Don't even think about it," Amelia said, noticing the longing in her eyes.

"I'll pay, of course," Britt replied, though she wasn't exactly sure with what. She'd spent the morning applying to any job that seemed remotely qualified for; jobs in Chicago, and as far away as San Diego or Atlanta. Surely, she'd hear something soon.

She licked her lower lip nervously. She wished she could be more confident about that.

"I won't be taking money from my sister," Amelia tutted. She began counting another tray, muttering under her breath until she reached two dozen. "It's the inventory I'm worried about. We're the only café in town with a booth, and even though a lot of people slip off to one of the local restaurants for a few hours during the day, last year we sold out of food by midafternoon."

"That's amazing!" Britt grinned at her sister, feeling proud of all that she'd accomplished. "You're a good businesswoman, Amelia."

Amelia snorted, but her cheeks flushed pink, betraying her own pride at the compliment. "I won't be if I don't get these trays to the town square in the next twenty minutes. Cora is setting up the booth, so she'll meet us over there." She hoisted one of the trays off the counter and made way for the back kitchen door that led out to a small parking alley where her car was parked. Even though the square was only three blocks from the café, Britt got the impression that her sister didn't want to take any risks of dropping the food, but when she saw the amount of food loaded into the back hatch of her sister's SUV, she changed her reasoning.

"There's enough to feed the entire town in here!" she exclaimed, looking at the plastic containers stacked high with cookies and sandwiches, all individually wrapped in waxed paper, tied with a simple bow of twine.

"That's the hope," Amelia said.

She stood back as Maddie slid the last of the sandwich trays into the trunk, and then closed it firmly. Maybe a little firmly, Britt thought, unless she was being overly sensitive.

Not feeding into it, Amelia blew out a breath, her eyes

bright. "Well, I've only got room for one passenger up front with me," she said, eyeing her sisters.

"I'll walk," Maddie volunteered, and given that she'd been at the café since possibly the crack of dawn to help finish up these items, it appeared that she needed a nap more than a walk. "And I'll lock up, too."

"See you there," Britt said with a smile as she climbed into the front seat beside Amelia. She was determined to wear Maddie down if it was the only thing she accomplished here in town. But at the rate things were going, she might have better luck turning the family business around than getting her youngest sister to warm up to her again.

"Do you think anything is up with Maddie?" Britt asked, once the doors were closed and Maddie was out of view.

Amelia blinked distractedly in her rearview mirror. "We're all just busy. This is a big day."

Of course. Maybe there really was nothing more to it than that.

"I mean what I said," Britt told her sister, looking at her until she forced her sister to meet her gaze. "You've accomplished a lot. And you know what you're doing. I've seen major corporations that have less business sense than you."

"I probably got it from Dad," Amelia said as she pulled onto the street. It was crowded, with everyone wanting to secure a spot near the square, but Amelia had promised she'd been offered a reserved spot, exclusively for the vendors. "We both do."

"About that..." Britt wasn't sure if she should even be bringing it up, but one look at her sister told her that Amelia wasn't even paying attention. She was cursing under her breath, the way she always did when she got behind the wheel, impatiently instructing the car in front of her to inch up rather than holding out for a spot on Main that they'd never fit into, and Britt could only smile and look out the window.

She'd forgotten how Amelia could be when she was driving. She'd forgotten a lot of things about the people in this town.

But then, she supposed, that had been the intention, hadn't it?

*

Amelia had been right in her prediction. And her concern. Within two hours, they'd already sold out of coffee and scones and by noon, half the sandwiches were gone, and the various pasta salads were going quickly. Maddie offered to run back to the café and make more, and Britt manned the counter until Cora came along and relieved her.

"You go enjoy yourself," Cora said, holding out a hand for the apron that Britt wore.

Britt hesitated. Working at the booth was an excuse to be here, but also to keep her distance from the social scene, and all who may be lingering in it. It was also a purpose, and for as long as she could remember, having a purpose and keeping busy was all that she knew.

"Why doesn't the orchard have a stand here?" she

asked aloud, thinking of how easy it would have been to put up a booth offering fresh cider and wine once the sun went down.

Amelia shrugged. "Beats me. I try to stay out of Dad's business. You know how set in his ways he is. And he knows best, doesn't he?"

Britt wasn't about to argue, not when there was a line from here to the big maple tree gathering impatiently. Her feet ached despite the comfortable shoes, and her stomach grumbled from lack of food because she hadn't found two minutes to eat when there were so many people that claimed to be hungrier than her waiting in line.

She untied her apron strings and handed it over to Cora.

"Call me if you need me," she said, stepping back from the counter.

She had been darting glances at the crowd all day, hoping to see Robbie almost as much as she hoped to miss him, but now she felt the need to seek him out. There was room for opportunity here that wasn't being tapped, and if her father wouldn't listen to her, then perhaps Robbie would be able to get through to him.

She wound her way through the crowds, pausing to greet the smiling faces she recognized, which were numerous, making small talk about all the exciting things that had kept her busy in Chicago—and away from Blue Harbor.

"It's so good to have you home," was the general sentiment, repeated over and over from everyone from her high school English teacher, now retired, to her cousins, whom she'd once considered nearly as close as her own sisters.

"Please tell me you're staying!" Jenna said as she leaned in for a hug. The youngest of Steve's daughters, she had the quietest personality and a good, genuine spirit that Britt had always been drawn to growing up. Unlike Maddie, who could be a handful when she was little, Jenna had been happy to sit and play dolls or let Britt style her hair.

Britt hated the thought of letting Jenna down. "I'll be here for at least the next two weeks."

At least? Why had she said that? Her smile slipped as Gabby picked up on the suggestion in her choice of wording, her eyes glimmering with interest.

"I need to find Robbie," Britt quickly said. "Have you seen him?"

Now Jenna and Gabby exchanged less than subtle glances. Gabby's smile was positively teasing. "Find Robbie? Is that so?"

"Stop," Britt warned. "It's just some…business stuff."

Gabby looked disappointed. "I think I saw him near the gazebo," she offered.

"Oh, look!" Jenna said sweetly. "Here comes your dad and that nice nurse taking care of him!"

Britt stiffened. The last thing she needed was to watch Candy flaunt her father all over the festival as if they were some sort of couple. With the promise to catch up with them later in the day and to of course stick around long enough to hear Jenna's entire concert, Britt excused herself.

Finally, she spotted Robbie, standing patiently near the part of the square carved out for games, watching as Keira's face was painted with streaks of pink and purple glittery paint.

"A unicorn?" she guessed, coming to stand beside him. He seemed to stiffen at her approach, but his expression relaxed into a smile when he caught her eye.

"It's a butterfly, I believe," he said mildly, giving Keira a doting smile.

"You came!" Keira cried out happily, as she bounded off the chair, pausing briefly to admire her painted cheeks in the mirror.

"I couldn't resist," Britt said. "I've actually been manning my sister's booth all morning." She turned to look up at Robbie as he watched Keira scamper ahead to check out the pie-eating contest.

"Why didn't Conway Orchard set up a booth for this event?" she asked.

He frowned down at her. "Have they ever hosted one before?"

"No," Britt said, at least, not to her knowledge. She hadn't been around the past few years to know what her father was or wasn't doing with the business, but now she realized that nothing had changed, or grown. And that maybe Amelia was right; he was too set in his ways to realize that if he wanted things to continue into the next generation, he'd have to adapt.

"It's a good idea," Robbie surprised her by saying. "Maybe he'd be interested in doing something next year."

The way he said that last sentence told Britt that he doubted this every bit as much as she did.

"I mean, look at all these people. And they're not just from Blue Harbor. It's a tourist event, too. And it pulls in other communities. We could introduce the cider to new people. Same with the wine." They came to a stop where the pie-eating contest was taking place, and she felt a burst of frustration building. "We could have sponsored the pies for the event."

"The pies are only sold at the market," Robbie pointed out. "And Maddie's got her hands full. She only does it because it's tradition."

"And no one has considered how to turn that into profit?" Britt countered. "This pie-eating contest is a great marketing opportunity!"

Now Robbie slid her a knowing look. "You've seen the books. Hate to break it to you, Britt, but the farm is hardly in a position to be giving things out for free. It's bad enough when the tours come through and people start eating the fruit right off the bushes."

He grinned at her to show that he was trying to make light of a difficult situation, but she struggled to feel the same.

"I used to love that pie-eating contest," she mused as she watched a little girl sink her face into a strawberry pie, her hands held firmly behind her back. She laughed to herself, imagining what she must have looked like, and knowing that she hadn't even cared at the time. She'd been light and carefree back then before the heaviness encroached and everything changed.

She patted her bun, making sure the chaos of the food stand hadn't made a mess of it.

"Oh, I remember," Robbie said, chuckling. "I never understood the draw myself. You never did tell me if you were doing it for the free pie or for the chance to win." He studied her for a moment. "But now I think I know the answer to that."

"Which is?" She folded her arms over her chest and blinked up at him, not sure she liked where this was heading, and not just because she had the uneasy feeling that they were entering a new zone, more than friendship, but not quite flirting.

"You like to win," he said. "You like to come out on top."

She had the distinct impression that this wasn't a compliment. "Doesn't everyone enjoy the thrill of victory? The rush of success?" She'd felt it every time she saw a company pulled from disorder. It was a feeling of power, but more than that, it was one of control, of knowing that she could right the wrongs. That sometimes, things didn't have to be as dire as they first appeared.

That something in this confusing, unsettling world could be made right again. That there was hope.

Robbie shrugged. "Some people just like the experience."

"Well, doing something just for the experience is a hobby," Britt countered. Her mind was back on the orchard, on all the avenues they could take, on all the ways they could tap into new markets and expand.

He whistled under his breath. "I thought we were talking about the pie-eating contest."

She opened her mouth to argue, and then shook her

head, grinning ruefully back at him. "You got me. Sorry. Force of habit."

"I thought you'd want to relax a bit. You're technically on vacation, aren't you?"

Britt swallowed hard, keeping her eyes fixed on the pie-eating contest, wondering if the girl with the strawberry pie would win and hoping, for some inexplicable reason, that she would.

She couldn't lie to Robbie. Not back then. Not now. Even if they weren't a couple anymore, and even if they maybe weren't even friends, she couldn't hide the truth from him. And she wasn't so sure that she wanted to, either. Robbie was the one person she had opened up to when life was hardest.

And he was just one of many people that she had shut out.

"I'm, um, on an extended vacation," she clarified, eyeing him. She could see the confusion knit his brow, so she added, "I got laid off. Ironic, isn't it? I advise companies on how to save their business, which sometimes results in letting go of people, and then I got a taste of my own medicine."

"I'm sorry, Britt," Robbie said, setting a hand on her arm. She didn't shrug it off, and despite the ache in her chest, she felt a laser focus on the softness of his touch and the sense of connection that had been missing from her life for so long. So achingly long.

She skirted her eyes around the grounds. "I haven't told my sisters yet. Or my Dad. He's trying to recover and there's been enough worry going around. Besides, I'm sure that something will turn up soon." She sniffed and lifted her chin. Still, a part of her stomach wavered, twisted and bubbling with nerves every time she dared to ask herself, what if something didn't turn up soon?

"Eager to get out of town, eh?" When he looked at her, she saw something close to hurt in his eyes, but he covered it quickly saying, "Your family has always been there for you, Britt. You wouldn't be worrying them. They'd probably be happy to help."

She nodded quietly, feeling the same shame and guilt creep up just as it did every time that she thought about the distance she'd put between herself and her sisters, and not just physically. "All the same. It's sort of a sore subject. Besides, maybe it's for the best that I'm out of a job right now."

He watched her carefully. "Now you have all the time you need to focus on the family business."

She nodded slowly. The business hadn't even been on her mind just then, but all the same, she said, "Yep. The business."

After all, she couldn't save her mother. She couldn't even save her relationship with Robbie. But maybe she could save the one thing that still tied her to this town and her childhood, the one positive thing that was still standing.

*

Robbie hadn't expected Britt to actually come to the event, but then, he hadn't expected her to still be in Blue Harbor either, or ever return for that matter. There had

been a time, when he'd first thought about coming back, that seeing her again had crossed his mind, even filled him with a flutter like something close to hope, but he'd closed that door, knowing it was pointless. That she wouldn't be back. And that he didn't care.

But she was back. And he did care. And he didn't know what to make of that.

"It's so nice to see the two of you together again!" Mrs. Foreman, who ran a B&B at the corner of Main Street and liked to keep tabs on all the happenings from her wraparound front porch, gushed as the sun began to set and the strings of lights that were hung from the trees popped on, illuminating the sky nearly as brightly as the stars that he'd missed so much out in Boston. Nothing beat the night sky of Blue Harbor, with its vast northern view.

Britt was quick to shake her head, her eyes bulging in alarm. "Oh, we're not—"

But Mrs. Foreman was having none of it. "I knew you'd both be back where you were meant to be eventually," she said with a little pat on Britt's hand.

To him, she gave a less than subtle wink, and both Britt and Robbie watched in silence as she walked away.

Britt guffawed loudly. "Well, that was—"

Robbie raised an eyebrow. "Typical?"

"I was going to say pushy, but typical works." Britt gave him a little smile. "It sure is different than life in the city. Everyone knows you. Everyone knows what you've been through." She sighed.

"Would it be strange to say that I kind of like that?"

Robbie admitted. He led her over to a bench under the oak tree before someone else could grab it. Keira was with her grandparents at the other end of the festival, and Jackson was no doubt tending bar at the inn, where he was happiest, or dodging the latest heart he'd broken.

"Why did you go?" Britt suddenly asked him. He was too caught off guard to answer right away and she leaned in, her voice low over the sound of the band that had just started playing, but loud enough to voice his biggest thoughts, and ones he asked himself, and questioned sometimes. But he always came back to the same answer. "Why'd you leave Blue Harbor all those years ago?"

He'd left. Taken a gap year. Then he'd stayed and gone to school in Boston and met Stephanie. And had Keira, he thought, watching as the little girl stepped out onto the dance floor, clapping her hands to something that had caught her attention.

"I left because you didn't come back," he said. He cleared his throat. There. It was out there. And it didn't matter now. He'd ended up where he was supposed to be. On the path that had brought him right back here.

Right next to Britt Conway.

He looked away again. At his daughter.

"You were supposed to go to Michigan State."

He nodded. "Guess you could say we're more alike than we thought back then." He slid her a glance and felt their eyes lock. "When you lose someone you love, sometimes it just hurts too much to stay."

"You could have come with me," Britt said quietly. She passed off her emotions with a casual shrug, but the strain in her eyes spoke differently. "Anyway," she said. "That was a long time ago. We've both moved on. Both changed."

"And now we're both back in Blue Harbor," he stated.

Britt gestured at something across the way. "I think your daughter is trying to get your attention."

Was she? Robbie shook his thoughts off Britt and turned toward the crowd to see Keira waving frantically in their direction. Only she wasn't trying to get Robbie's attention at all. It was Britt she was calling out to now.

"I think she wants to show you her painting," Robbie said. He leaned in until he was close enough to feel the heat from Britt's skin, catch the faint scent of peony that was her favorite fragrance back when they'd dated. Not much had changed after all, despite what she insisted.

Or what he'd hoped.

"In case you can't tell at first glance, the painting is of an elephant," he whispered.

She looked up at him, and he wondered if she would pull back, if he'd overstepped and gotten too comfortable. But she grinned, all the way up to her eyes, and said, "Did you guess wrong?"

He laughed. "I may have complimented her beautiful painting of a snow-capped mountain."

Britt shook her head, but she was smiling as she walked away. "Elephant. Got it."

Robbie stayed back, watching as Britt walked toward his daughter, her hair bouncing in its ponytail, the skirt of her dress swishing at her knees. Gone were the rigid skirts and formal tops. From this view, she was the same old Britt.

Nope. Nothing had really changed at all.

"Having fun?" He turned to see his mother approach, her look a little too coy for his liking.

"Keira's having a good time," he replied. That was all that mattered anymore.

"She seems to have found a new friend," his mother said, her tone laced with suggestion, but her meaning was a mystery to him.

They'd moved on from the art display to the craft table, and Robbie's jaw tightened as he watched Keira show Britt how to assemble the paper lanterns that everyone would light and release over the lake upon sundown, even though he was fairly certain that Britt knew how to do it herself. It was town tradition, after all, and she hadn't been away long enough to have forgotten.

He hadn't, he thought, swallowing hard.

"There's nothing going on, if that's what you're insinuating, Mom," he said gently.

"I'm just saying," Bonnie said delicately. "It wouldn't be so bad if something were. Keira's having a good time like you said, but it's okay for you to have a good time, too."

She gave him a little pat on the arm as she walked away to join a group of her friends he recognized from her bridge club.

Across the green, Keira caught his eye and waved at him, her face beaming and her smile wide enough to light up her eyes, even from the distance.

His daughter was having a good time. And with Britt.

And he wasn't so sure how he felt about that.

9

Britt pressed her ear to the door of her father's study before gingerly turning the knob, bracing herself for the sight of entangled limbs or Candy's bouncy blonde curls dangling over her father's grinning face. She nearly shivered at the image.

Instead, she let out a sigh of relief when she saw that the room was empty. No Candy. But no sight of her father, either. Frowning, her relief quickly turned to anxiety as she crossed the hall to the side window of the dining room and saw that Candy's car wasn't parked in its usual spot beside her own. Had she somehow managed to get Britt's father down the porch steps and into the car? It was possible but risky. Was there a doctor's appointment Britt didn't know about? But it was Sunday morning. Doctor offices weren't open.

Her chest seized when she considered something worse. A run to the hospital. Cardiac arrest from clogged arteries from all of Candy's cheese biscuits.

Or over-stimulation.

Please no, she thought, squeezing her eyes tight.

Maybe he'd injured himself. Maybe someone had crashed into him at the festival yesterday, just as she'd feared. Or maybe her father had fallen out of bed or fallen trying to get to the bathroom in the middle of the night.

Or trying to do something else that usually takes place in the dark, she thought, narrowing her eyes.

She went quickly back to the kitchen and directly to the fridge, where Candy had taken to leaving notes containing inspirational messages on the door under magnets collected over the years, but the only thing that today's notecard said was, "Bloom where you are planted." Hardly original, and Britt couldn't help but wonder if there was a hint of suggestion in Candy choosing that phrase. Then again, yesterday Candy had tacked up a quote about living in the moment, so maybe she was just running low on ideas lately.

She called out her father's name, sensing as she did that the house was empty. It was old and creaky, and even from upstairs, there was a different feel to the home when it was occupied. Growing up, the back door seemed to swing open and closed all day long in the summer, with all four of them bounding in and out from the lake to the kitchen to grab more snacks or drinks.

She shook her head at the thought of it now. Her mother claimed she never tired of the energy of the house, and Britt remembered not knowing what she meant until it all changed. The house that was once so full of life became quiet and still. And now, well, now it was most certainly empty.

She went out the same back door that her mother used to laughingly say was about to fall off its hinges, finding her father in one of the old rocking chairs on the back porch, looking out over the water, a cup of coffee warming his hands. It was a clear summer day, and already there were boats out on the lake. Sails were down, though; not enough breeze in the air.

"I couldn't find you," she said a little breathlessly. Her chest felt tight, even now, when he was right here within arm's reach, and she dropped onto the chair beside him, resisting the urge to fling her arms around his neck, the way she had done when she was a little girl.

Didn't want to go injuring him when she'd been so concerned about that happening, after all.

He gave her a mild smile. "I'm right here. I'll always be right here, Britt."

She nodded. She supposed she'd always known that. And counted on it. And maybe, she thought, taken it for granted.

"Candy went out?" She knew the answer but thought it best to confirm the fact.

"Went to run some errands," Dennis replied. "Don't worry. She won't be back for a couple of hours. She's having her hair done."

So Britt's suspicions were correct. That curious shade of blonde was not Candy's natural color.

She immediately wanted to take back the unkind sentiment when she saw the knowing look her father was giving her. "I know you don't like her."

"It's not that I don't like her," Britt interjected. "I don't even know her."

"Exactly. You aren't even giving her a chance." Her father shrugged and returned his eyes to the water. "Maybe I expected too much. But you aren't little anymore. None of you are. And..."

And a lot of things, she thought, studying the frown of his profile. This house was big. And it was now empty, and it wasn't ever meant to be that way, she knew. Her father wasn't getting any younger. And he had found someone who made him happy. Someone who couldn't be more different than her mother, who was lovely and graceful and quiet and unassuming. Britt didn't know what to make of that.

"Maybe I'm the one who isn't open to change," she said slowly, thinking of Amelia's words, that their father was stubborn and set in his ways. "I guess that it was easier to stay away, to think of this house, and this town, the way it used to be. It's hard to face it now. Seeing how it's all so different."

"But you're different too," her father pointed out. "All buttoned up and closed off. Not that I blame you. I just...well, sometimes I miss that sweet girl who used to throw her arms around my neck and show up a little later than curfew."

Britt felt a lump building in her throat. She missed that girl too. But that girl's spirit had died along with her mother. And had been lost without Robbie.

"I grew up," she said tightly, but they both knew it was much more than that. She'd grown, but not into the person she wanted to be. Her father was right; she didn't show her heart anymore. She didn't live with abandon. How could she? She kept a tight schedule, she lived for routine. She kept people at arm's length. She didn't get close.

She'd thought that she was better off that way. Now, she wasn't so sure. Her sisters were all still close, and seemingly content with their lives. And Maddie wasn't even really speaking to her.

And she had the distinct feeling that she had missed out on…something. Because there was certainly nothing waiting for her in Chicago. No husband. No boyfriend. Not even a real friend.

"I'm proud of you," her father said, grinning. He pulled in a breath as he glanced over at her as if preparing himself for what he was about to say next. "I suppose you'll be getting back to the city soon?"

She licked her bottom lip. Now it was her turn to look out over the water. The view never failed to calm her, to give her something to focus on, when the world around her seemed too overwhelming. Along the shoreline she could see children splashing in the water, squealing at its icy temperatures. It wouldn't warm up until about August, but that had never stopped her as a kid, had it?

Now it would. Now everything seemed to stop her.

"You'll be back on your feet soon," she said, dodging his direct question. The truth was that she wasn't so sure that she'd be back in Chicago in two weeks. She wasn't renewing the lease on her apartment, and she hadn't heard back from any more of the jobs she'd applied to yet. Would she go back, stay in a month-to-month studio apartment until a job opened up? There didn't seem to be much point in that.

Dennis tented his fingers in his lap. "Conway Orchard has been in the family for generations. I love the place.

But with Steve retired, and that fall I took, well…call me crazy, but a part of me was hoping that I might pass on the reins soon."

Britt frowned at him. Retire? But her father loved to work. Since her mother had died, she could even say that he lived to work.

"Pass on the reins? To Robbie?" Robbie was passionate, and he was good at what he did. But he wasn't family. He could have been, in another life. If things had gone differently.

She shut that thought away. Robbie had made it clear he had no regrets, and why should he? He had a sweet little girl. And she had…nothing. Not even a job anymore.

Her father was silent, one eyebrow raised as he stared at her, and she felt a sinking, twisting feeling in her stomach as the realization took hold, remembering what Robbie had said, wondering if her father did too. Once she had dreamed of taking over the business, sure, but things had changed.

"Oh, Dad," she said, her heart heavy with regret. There was nothing worse than disappointing her father when all she wanted to do was to protect him. She could never forget the ache in her chest when she stood at his side at her mother's funeral, seeing him so lost that she barely recognized him, not knowing what to do at the moment other than take his hand, knowing it wasn't going to be enough.

"Just something to think about," he said, holding up a hand. "If you ever decide to come home to stay, you've got more than your family waiting here for you. You're like me, Britt. You like to keep busy. And none of your sisters love that orchard the way you did."

Tears burned the back of her eyes. There was so much she wanted to say, so much that hadn't been said, that she couldn't bring herself to say when she was younger and hadn't said over the years out of guilt and shame and confusion. It was all there, bursting to come out, but all she could say was, "Dad."

She reached out to take his hand, again because it seemed to be all that she knew to do, and he squeezed it tight, looking firmly in her eyes.

"It was just a thought. What I want is for you to be happy. Like I said, I'm always here. I'm not going anywhere."

She gave a watery smile as he leaned back in his chair and looked out over the lake.

He'd always been here. And she hadn't. And she wanted to believe his words and his promise. Almost as much as she wished she could give him the one thing he was asking her for.

*

Robbie told himself that he wasn't dodging Britt, but when she slipped over to the office building after the market was over, he couldn't postpone an interaction any longer. He stopped by his desk and gathered up the folders containing vendor information and details of last year's Cherry Festival and walked down to the hall to Britt's office. Make that Dennis's office. In the week since she'd arrived, the space already felt different, more inviting, and not just because of the lingering scent of her perfume which brought him back to a time and a place when he was completely carefree and content.

He reminded himself that in just two weeks it would be back to the way it was. Britt would be gone and all would return to normal.

But more and more, normal was starting to feel lonely. Dennis was a good boss who treated his staff well, but he was a quiet man, and not one to discuss big ideas. He had a system, and everyone followed it. The work day was usually uneventful, but it kept Robbie busy enough, before he spent a few hours in the evening with Keira, and then lingered in his empty house, hoping the television would pass for company.

He knocked on Britt's open door, feeling his stomach tighten as she looked up from her paperwork and grinned at him. Her eyes were wide and alert, and despite the overly formal attire and fierce styling of her hair, for a moment, she looked as fresh-faced and youthful as the girl he'd once loved, and he had to clear his throat and snap himself back to the present and the reason that he was here at all.

"I thought that since it's quiet and we're both here that we'd better go over the plans for the Cherry Festival," he said.

She nodded and motioned for him to take a seat on the other side of the desk. Then, on second thought, she stood up. "It's a weekend, and I didn't stop for lunch. Want to discuss this over at the café? Company's treat, since it's a business meeting."

A business meeting. In other words, not a date. He supposed he should be relieved that she insisted on clarifying that, but it didn't make him feel any less conflicted when he shrugged and said, "Sure."

Keira was spending the day at the inn today, helping his mother garden in the small backyard where guests could sit with a coffee under the big maple trees, and he could swing by and pick her up while he was in town. They took his truck; Britt explained that she was happy to walk back and take in the fresh air, and he kept the conversation light and on the topic of the Cherry Festival on the brief journey into town. His eyes were firmly on the road, not on the long bare legs that were poking out of her tight navy skirt, because despite the hair, she was hell-bent on dressing the part of a corporate executive, instead of remembering where she was. Who she was. It felt strange to have someone other than Keira in the vehicle, and she sat in the back, where he could check on her through the rearview mirror. The passenger seat was always empty now, other than the few times he gave his brother a lift somewhere.

The café was crowded, but then, it was an early Sunday afternoon, and Amelia barely suppressed her surprise at the sight of them walking up to the counter together. Her blue eyes were round as she stared at her sister, as if waiting for some sort of explanation that could be communicated without any words.

Britt said pointedly, "We're here to discuss the Cherry Festival. Can you send over two coffees and a plate of whatever you recommend?"

Amelia looked mildly disappointed, but said, "Of course. I just made a batch of cheddar scones. Fresh from the oven. And Maddie dropped off two pies on her way to the market this morning. I still have a few slices left if you're interested. We close at two on Sundays, but you're welcome to linger as long as you please." Her eyes gleamed.

"I didn't realize that Maddie sold pies here," Britt said tersely.

"Only on Sundays," Amelia said. "And not every Sunday. Just when I ask extra nicely." She grinned and promised to have their order up shortly.

Britt waited until she and Robbie were settled at a table near the window to say, "I actually wanted to discuss Maddie with you. I think that we should ask her to make pies. For the festival." They'd already discussed the usual setup for the event, and Britt had mentioned on the ride into town that she was hoping to increase traffic by offering a raffle this year.

He narrowed his eyes on her. "You're not suggesting a pie-eating contest?"

She laughed. "I'm suggesting we see how people like the pies. They sell out every week at the market. It's an opportunity to test new products with a bigger audience."

"New product? Britt, there hasn't been a new product in over a decade. Your father likes to sink his time into what he knows works. Even with the wines."

"And I think the pies will work. Why not? They sell well. People have always loved them. We're in the business of fruit."

"But we have no inventory," Robbie pointed out, thinking of how many people had attended the Cherry Festival last year and knowing that Britt was determined to increase that number this year by offering hayrides, cherry pit spitting contests (even she had to laugh about that one), and an entire craft section for the kids, which he knew Keira would appreciate. "How many pies were you thinking?"

"Well, we have three weeks," Britt countered. "Besides, I think that Maddie needs a new challenge. Working here at the café is great for her, but she needs something for herself."

Robbie leaned back in his chair. "Is this whole pie idea personal or professional?" Seeing the flare of pink rise up in Britt's cheeks, he quickly said, "I mean, are you doing this for your sister, or for the business?"

Britt blinked at him. "Business, though I suppose it can be both. Her pies sell out every single Sunday, without fail. No other product has the same success. Maybe that's something to consider. When we look to the future."

He raised an eyebrow. "Future?"

"Of the business, of course," Britt said.

Business. Of course. Robbie pulled in a breath, hiding the disappointment that had no business there.

Britt paused as the sister she was speaking of approached with two cups of steaming coffee.

"Scones will be right up," Maddie said, before dashing off again.

Britt added a splash of cream to her coffee and took a

sip. "You've tasted those pies," she said in a low voice that caused him to lean across the table, closing the distance between them. "It's the very same recipe that my…" She took another sip of coffee, not finishing that thought.

She didn't need to. Robbie knew. Better than anyone. And not just because he'd experienced loss firsthand, but because he'd been there, at Britt's side. He'd known her mother. It was another example of how unfair and unpredictable life could be.

"Everyone loves those pies," he agreed. He gave her a sad smile. "Everyone always did."

She met his eyes, and he saw the gratitude that shone in them. He cleared his throat, happy to be distracted by the arrival of Amelia now bringing them a plate of four scones and what appeared to be some canapés, too.

"I need you to taste these for me. If you like them, I plan to serve them at Jenna's birthday party this Friday."

Britt looked up at her quizzically. "Jenna's party? Was I invited?"

Amelia laughed. "You're more than invited. You're expected." She patted her sister on the shoulder. "Sorry, I didn't mention it before you came back, because, well, you know. But I assumed one of our sisters had mentioned it by now. I'm hosting it at my place. Seven sharp. Sorry, Robbie, but girls only for this one."

Britt's cheeks flared a deep shade of pink, and Robbie relieved her by saying, "I'm sure my brother will be sorry to miss it. Between us, I think he has a little crush on Gabby."

Britt seemed to compose herself and said, "Name someone who doesn't!"

He could think of one. Gabby was pretty, but she had never appealed to him the way that Britt had, with her contagious laugh and earnest way of listening.

Amelia set a bag on the table in front of him.

"For Keira," she said with a grin.

He didn't have to look inside to know that it was probably her favorite cookie that she asked for every time they stopped by the café. Maddie made them just for Keira, he suspected.

"Thank you," he said. "And Maddie. She'll be thrilled. I'll have to bribe her to wait until after dinner to eat it."

"There's one in there for you, too," Amelia added. "Life is better in pairs."

She gave a suggestive look at Britt and then sauntered away with a little smile, leaving Britt sitting silently at the table, her face burning.

"Excuse them," she said.

"I've been getting the same encouragement from my family," he admitted.

Britt's eyes flicked to his before she took another sip of the coffee. "So you're on board? With the pies?"

"I think it's up to Maddie," he said. He tore apart a scone, so flaky and buttery that it nearly melted in his mouth.

Britt hesitated for a moment before leaning across the table. "I get the impression that Maddie is upset with me. I'm not even sure how to talk to her anymore." She shrugged and leaned back in her chair, clutching her coffee mug with both hands. "Well, she can't take offense to this. Who doesn't want to hear that there is more demand for their product? I'm sure she'll appreciate a pay increase."

Robbie watched Britt carefully, wondering just when things had changed. When she had hardened herself, made everything about numbers and facts, and not about people themselves.

But he knew the answer to that. He knew best of all, really.

"Remind me before I go that I need to place an order for two dozen of these cookies," he said, suddenly remembering the class party he had volunteered for—make that, been volunteered for. If it was up to Natalie Clark, he would have partnered with her for decorations, but he'd managed to put his name down for the cookie tray instead.

Britt arched an eyebrow. "Two cookies aren't enough for dessert?"

"Class party for the last day of school," he explained. "Keira wanted to bake something, but—"

"But why not? It's not that hard!" She read his expression and said, "Well, not everyone can make cookies and scones this good, but I'm sure you could pull something together. Besides, if you bring a tray of cookies from here, everyone will know where they're from. They're one of a kind."

She had a point. Still, he was barely getting the hang of anything that wasn't cooked on the grill on his deck. Baking seemed out of his league just yet.

"I'm happy to help. When is the last day of school?"

"Friday," he said. He pulled in a breath. It was a generous offer, and he knew that Keira would be thrilled. And for that reason alone, he should probably think of a polite excuse.

But he didn't want to take that joy away from his daughter. And truth be told, he liked spending time with Britt again. And it was just cookies.

"I'll even bring the ingredients," she said. "I may not have the same talent as two of my sisters when it comes to the kitchen, but I know my way around a recipe, and well, it would get me out of the house."

He grinned. "Your dad's girlfriend still bothering you?"

"It's not his girlfriend," she said testily. She hesitated. Tore at the corner of a scone but didn't eat it. "My dad had a talk with me." She glanced at him, looking uncertain. "He wants me to take over the business. In his place."

A strange mix of emotions muddled together until Robbie couldn't form a coherent response. Britt in Blue Harbor full time? He hadn't dared to think of it. Somehow, it was easier spending time with her like this knowing that it was limited. Safer.

"Did you tell him about your job?" he asked.

She shook her head and glanced toward the counter, where Amelia was busy chatting with a customer. "No. He brought it up when I mentioned him returning to work."

"And are you…considering it?" he asked.

"Well, I have to consider all my options at this point, don't I?" she said. "And being back here isn't easy, but...it's made me realize how much I was missing being away."

He could tell by the regret in her eyes that was she was referring to more than her cousin's birthday party. That, maybe, she was referring to Maddie, who had definitely seemed a bit chilly toward Britt at the farmer's market this morning, if anyone were to ask him.

He nodded his head, trying to think of what this would mean for him. If Britt was back in town, working with him at the farm every day, like they had for the past week.

Now wasn't the time for thinking of that, he told himself. She'd left town once before, without warning, or even care. She'd done what was best for her. He understood that. Understood that he wasn't it.

And she wasn't what was best for him, either. What was best for him, and for his daughter, was to keep things as they were. They were happy. And they were fine. Or they would be. Someday.

10

On Thursday evening, Britt pulled her car to a stop outside the address that Robbie had given her, even though she already knew the house. She knew every house in Blue Harbor—it was a small enough town without any new construction that you knew the landmarks, like the yellow Colonial on the bend up toward the bluffs, or the large white Victorian with the clear view of Evening Island, and a wraparound porch dotted with rocking chairs, owned by old Lottie Erickson and in the family for generations.

Robbie's house was two blocks off the lakefront: a small grey cottage that had once belonged to Britt's childhood friend Rebecca's grandparents. She'd never been inside but remembered that at Christmastime, the Dodsons would put a candle in every window and hang a cheerful wreath on the front door secured by a thick red velvet bow.

It seemed strange to think of Robbie living here now. With a daughter. The last time she'd seen him, he had still been a teenager, living in the coach house which was his family home, just behind the inn his parents owned in the center of town.

He opened the door before she had even reached to

knock, wearing jeans that skimmed his bare feet, and his work shirt untucked and rolled at the sleeves. They had both been too busy to see each other much this week. Britt was still going over the financials, trying to come up with a strategy to get the business on better footing, and Robbie had been meeting with vendors in town for the upcoming Cherry Festival.

"Nice house. You're such an adult," she said, giving him a little smile.

He cocked an eyebrow. "And you're not?"

She supposed it was true, that to the outsider, she may look like she knew what she was doing, that she had her life in order. That she had—*had* being the operative word here—a big career.

"Don't you have a fancy place in the city?" When he caught the look on her face, he explained, "Your dad brags about you a lot."

"If you call original plumbing in a vintage walk-up *fancy*," she said with a smile. She had always wanted to get around to putting more into the décor, but she'd never quite dared to trust that it would ever be home, or permanent.

Now it would be so much easier to pack everything up and move. Most of her clothes were folded in a suitcase anyway, ready to go on the next long business trip. Ready to leave at a moment's notice.

But where would she go next?

The bubble of anxiety that bloomed in her stomach disappeared when Keira's smiling face appeared in a doorway. "You're here!"

She said it as if it were a surprise, as if she hadn't been so sure that Britt would come at all, and at that moment, Britt felt an instant connection with the little girl, and a desire to please her. Like Britt, she had lost her mother. Her world had been suddenly uprooted. Her life forever changed. The future was uncertain. But some things, well, some things you could count on.

She glanced up at Robbie as he let her pass by him and closed the door behind them. He was giving her a funny look, his mouth pulling into a smile as his eyes roamed her face. "What is that for?"

"Your hair," he said, motioning to the loose locks that fell at her shoulders. "It looks nice."

Britt blushed, warming at the compliment. "Thanks."

"It looks better than nice, Dad," Keira corrected, with an exaggerated look in his direction. "It looks beautiful!"

Britt laughed, but Robbie just grinned a little wider. "You're right, Keira. It looks beautiful."

The air trapped in her lungs for a moment, and the three of them stood in the hallway lit by the evening sunlight that came in through the large windows at the back of the house, where Britt could already see a cookbook spread out on the butcher block countertop.

"I brought some ingredients," she said, letting Robbie take the grocery bags from her.

"How much do I owe you?" he asked, but she held up a hand.

"Consider us even." She squared him with a look.

"You're the one doing me a favor tonight, in case you're forgetting." He motioned toward Keira, who was already scampering back to the kitchen. Britt could make out the sounds of drawers opening and closing.

"When I left my house tonight, Candy was spoon-feeding *Denny* a bowl of ice cream," Britt said, sparking a mischievous grin from Robbie.

"Denny?"

Her eyes hooded. "Don't even get me started. You'd think the man couldn't do anything for himself. Between you and me, I'm starting to think that he's milking this injury."

"Well, he did break his arm," Robbie pointed out.

"Not his right arm," Britt said on a sigh. She pursed her lips. No sense in thinking about that just now. She had baking to do. And she craved the thought of staying busy all night if it meant keeping her mind from wandering to things she'd rather not worry about.

She skirted a glance toward Robbie. Well, most things.

With that, she walked down the hall to the bright and sunny kitchen, where Keira was already standing with a wooden spoon in one hand and a mixing bowl in the other.

Robbie and Britt laughed. "I can see you're all ready!" Britt said.

"She's been looking forward to this all day," Robbie replied, a little tightly. He set the grocery bags on the counter, and Britt helped him unpack the ingredients while she looked around the room. The fridge was covered with drawings and paintings, a picture of Keira down by the lake, another on a barstool that Britt recognized from the inn.

She pulled her eyes back to the counter before she saw too much. There was bound to be a picture of Stephanie in here somewhere, after all, and even though she was Keira's mother, and even though she was gone, it still felt awkward to think that Robbie had loved another woman.

Especially when she had never loved another man.

"So, what are we making?" Robbie asked, looking at her expectantly.

Her voice caught in her throat as she stared back at him. She had naively assumed that it would be just she and Keira baking tonight, that Robbie wasn't interested, not just incapable. But now she saw the eager gleam in his eye and the hopeful expression on Keira's face, and she realized that, of course, this would be a family event. Not that she was part of this family.

She wasn't really part of any family. Not anymore.

"Well, I thought we could make some strawberries and cream cupcakes. It's a recipe that my mom always used to make for my birthday each year, at my request, even though strawberries were out of season by then." She didn't know why she had volunteered that information, or even mentioned her mother when normally it hurt too much to even think of her, but she'd settled on the recipe because it was the best one that she knew, and one of the only things she'd ever baked, once a year, in the kitchen alone with her mother. Their special time.

"That sounds delicious," Robbie said, walking around the kitchen island to wash his hands at the sink.

She swallowed hard and forced a bright smile. "I brought enough to make a double batch, for my cousin's birthday party tomorrow night." Though she could only assume that Amelia would have most of the food covered, she didn't want to show up empty-handed.

"It's my birthday this weekend too!" Keira said excitedly as she clambered onto a stool. "We're having a tea party this Saturday, with pink sparkly crowns, and I have a pink dress to wear, and Daddy said he will even put my hair in pigtails that aren't lopsided."

"*Try* to put your hair in pigtails that aren't lopsided," Robbie warned.

"Can you come?" Keira blinked up at her with big eyes, and Britt skirted a nervous glance in Robbie's direction. He looked as caught off guard as she felt.

"Oh," she said, wincing back at Keira. "I probably have to work on Saturday, honey."

Keira's expression immediately fell, but she nodded her head. "Okay."

Britt looked at Robbie, who had shoved his hands into his pockets and was frowning pensively at his daughter.

"You're welcome to stop by," he suddenly said. "After work."

She hadn't planned on going to work, and he knew it, of course. Although, she might have done if Candy got out one more tub of that ice cream and sang out to her father that she had something almost sweeter for him than candy...followed by her trill of laughter at her own joke.

Besides, the plans for the Cherry Festival were shaping up nicely. She was excited about the changes. She could go to work... But the thought of going to Keira's party sounded like a lot more fun.

Keira looked at Britt hopefully. "Can you?"

Britt shared a small smile with Robbie, telling herself that he was just trying to keep his daughter happy, that there was absolutely nothing more to it than that.

"I wouldn't miss it," she said.

After all, she'd missed enough already.

*

The cupcakes were frosted and set up on a cooling rack, with strict instructions from Britt to pack them in the container she had provided, so they wouldn't get smashed en route to school.

"Yes, Boss," Robbie joked, even though the truth of it was that he probably would have done just that. The only plastic containers he owned were left over from the various casseroles that Natalie liked to drop off. He knew that he should probably give those back. That she was no doubt hoping that he would give them back. That it would give them another chance to talk, an opportunity for her to invite him in, and he didn't want to go in. He didn't want to get inside another woman's world.

But that wasn't the case with Britt, was it?

She was in his world right now. And she fit in nicely.

"It was nice of you to share that recipe," he said as she tucked away the book she'd brought with her.

"It was nice making it," Britt admitted. She gave him a little smile. "It's been a long time since I've had any memories of the past. Tasting those cupcakes, well…it was almost like having her here, just for a moment."

"Sort of like Maddie's pies," he said.

Britt tipped her head. "Thanks for reminding me. I haven't had a moment alone with Maddie, and I'm hoping to discuss things with her tomorrow night at the party."

"You really think those pies are the way to turn the business around?"

"I think it's a step in the right direction," Britt said. "We need to expand our product line. Either that or cut down."

His eyes flashed on her. "You mean let people go?"

She shrugged. "What other choice is there?"

He shook his head firmly. "Your father wouldn't allow it."

"My father is planning to retire. Whoever takes over that business will need to make some major changes, if anyone wants to buy it as it now stands."

"Some of those people have been with the business for longer than you and I have been alive."

"And I sincerely hope it doesn't come to that!" Britt sighed and leaned against the counter. "Look, I'm not trying to upset you. I'm just trying to be practical and think of a way to increase profits."

"At the risk of losing the heart of the business?" Robbie frowned. He saw Britt's point, of course he did, but it just wasn't that easy. This wasn't Chicago, or a big city, where you didn't know half the people you crossed on the street. Dory was a prime example of someone who was more than just a coworker. She had brought him a casserole every single Sunday for eight straight weeks when he and Keira first moved back to town.

"It's like you said the other day at the café," Britt said. "It's business. Not personal."

"No," he said, shaking his head. "I suppose it isn't." But he intended to make her see that it was.

Keira had gone upstairs to put on pajamas when they'd started cleaning up the mess, and now Robbie took the opportunity to make an excuse and leave the room to check on her. Somehow, it was almost easier with his daughter present, serving as a buffer, as a reminder of his role in life and the stance that he had taken. But the more he saw how engaged Keira was with Britt, how she lit up in her presence and giggled a bit more than usual, how Britt seemed to interact with her with ease, the more he also grew uneasy, thinking of how impossible it would be protect his daughter, and that he wasn't so sure he knew how to anymore.

Keira's door was closed, and he could see light coming through the space underneath. He knocked quietly before turning the handle, releasing a sigh when he saw that she was already sound asleep, on top of her cover, curled up next to her favorite stuffed animal.

It was late, he knew, and the excitement had no doubt tired her out. Carefully he pulled down her pink and purple floral printed quilt and picked her up before placing her head down on her pillow. She stirred for a moment before murmuring, "Thank you, Daddy," and he knew, by the little smile on her mouth, that she wasn't referring to being tucked in under a warm blanket.

She was referring to Britt. He'd invited her into his kitchen. Into his home. But was he really ready to invite her into his life? To break down the shell that she had put up, even though he'd already seen some cracks in her armor…especially when she was with Keira.

Britt was admiring a photo of Keira on the mantle when he came back down, unsure of what to do next until he saw her, standing in his home, a home he had never shared with Stephanie. A home that had felt so lonely so many nights at this hour, when Keira was asleep and the rooms felt too quiet, the space too empty, and there was nothing but the sound of the television or his thoughts to keep him company.

But tonight that wasn't the case. And as much he didn't want to admit it, he felt better than he had in a long time.

"Wine?" he asked before he had time to process what came next.

Britt set the photo back in its place and nodded. "That would be nice. But just one. I'm driving."

"I suppose you don't drive much in the city," he said as he reached for a bottle from the cabinet. For a moment, his hands hovered over the special bottles, the ones he hadn't dared to open just yet, the ones he was saving, for what day he wasn't sure exactly, and he took one of the orchard's favorites instead, their best seller, and grabbed two glasses while he was at it.

"No, but when I'm on the road I do." She took her glass from him after he'd filled it. "Do you ever miss city life?"

He thought about it for a moment and then shook his head. "No. Can't say that I do. And not for the reasons that you think. Stephanie…" Here he caught her eye and paused. It felt strange discussing his wife with Britt.

When her expression didn't waver, he dared to con-

tinue. "Stephanie liked the city. She was a costume designer, and it worked for her, professionally. We argued about it, the trade-offs of a commute versus a life in the burbs. Then, after…Well, I wrestled with it. I wanted to be sure I was doing what was best for Keira. She'd had enough change in her life, and I didn't want to disrupt things further. Boston was the only home she had ever known."

Britt nodded as they settled onto the sofa. It was new—he hadn't wanted to keep too much of the furnishings from their apartment in Boston. It was easier that way, starting fresh.

Starting over.

"Keira seems happy here in town," Britt said.

"She is. Being around my family, making friends, having a yard out back…"

Britt gave him a little smile. "I sense a hesitation."

There was a hesitation. A big one. One that he hadn't considered before, because it had been easier then, to put up a wall, to tell himself he was better off alone. Happier that way.

And then Britt had to waltz back into town. And into his life.

"I want what's best for her," he said. "I thought if we moved back to town, close to family, and got settled into a routine, that everything would be okay."

"But?" Britt gave him a little smile.

He swallowed hard. "I told myself that Keira already had a mother. That she didn't need a new female figure in her life."

"Is that what's best for her? Or best for you?" Britt asked, arching an eyebrow.

He grinned at her ruefully. "You sound like my mother."

Or like someone who cared about him.

"Or…like a friend?" Her tone was teasing, but the look in her eyes said something deeper was behind her words. That maybe, she felt the same things that he did.

He leaned forward as if it was the most natural thing in the world, and in many ways, it was. This was Britt. Britt whom he chased through the orchard, and Britt whom he held in his arms. Britt whom he stood by on her hardest days, holding her hand, saying nothing. Britt whom he watched drive away in the back of her father's car that hot summer day.

She was there. The same girl she had always been, but it seemed she was fighting that nearly as much as he was.

"Daddy?"

Robbie stiffened and pulled back, turning to see Keira in the doorway, rubbing her eyes.

"I can't find Cocoa," she said, referring to the stuffed toy which, sure enough, was flopped on the armchair.

"I should go," Britt said a little breathlessly, setting her wine glass on the coffee table.

He wanted to protest, but she was probably right. She should go because if she stayed, he might do something he shouldn't.

Like fall for Britt Conway all over again.

11

The sun that shone all day Friday, keeping Robbie out in the fields, rather than at his desk, was replaced with clouds and the threat of rain by the time Britt arrived on Amelia's doorstep that night, suddenly wishing she had driven over rather than walked.

It had been a quiet day, and Britt had kept busy sifting through the rest of her father's files, jotting down strategies for paying off the loan and giving them a financial cushion, even though none seemed like an ideal option. The Cherry Festival was the biggest opportunity they had, and without much time left, she went through her notes from her meeting with Robbie and made a secondary list of all the tasks they would need to delegate or be responsible for in order to make this event the success she intended it to be.

Still, as she read over the bullet points of all the little things that were needed to bring this festival together, from the ponies for the rides, to the face painters, to the buckets of cherry pits, and the band, she couldn't help but think how much more fulfilling it had been to plan it with Robbie. She was used to this kind of solitude, even enjoyed it in the past, but today she found herself restless and lonely and looking very forward to the promise of some company tonight.

Now, she shifted the container of strawberries and cream cupcakes to one hand and knocked with the other. The door burst open seconds later, and Amelia's cheeks were flushed as she ushered her inside.

"You beat the rain!" Amelia took one glance up at the sky before closing the door firmly. She walked purposefully down the narrow hall to the kitchen, where trays and platters of food were all set up. Through the opening to the living room, Britt could see candles set up on the coffee table and bunches of balloons on either side of the hearth. "I had plans to set up the back deck, but looks like we'll be indoors instead. Maddie's starting a fire. You never know if a cold front will blow through."

It was true that the evenings could be unexpectedly cool through June this far north, and the lake effect didn't help matters. Another thing that Britt had failed to consider when she set out for the evening. At least Amelia would happily lend her a sweater. And an umbrella.

"This is a lovely home," she said, taking in the small but cozy quarters.

"It's not much," Amelia said, but Britt could tell that she was pleased.

"It's lovely," Britt said again, venturing into the living room, and she meant it. Looking around, she saw the personal touches that reflected Amelia's style and warm personality. There were cheerful throw pillows on the couch, and a cozy blanket in a soft shade of blue draped over the arm of the chair, a pedestal table at its side that held a stack of books, a lamp, and a picture frame of all of the sisters when they were younger.

She glanced at Maddie, who was just rolling back onto her heels and standing. "Hey, Maddie!" She grinned at her sister, who gave a tight smile in return.

Pushing away her frustration, she held out her container to Amelia. "Strawberries and cream cupcakes," she said because she knew that Amelia was curious. It wasn't like Britt to bake, but she didn't want to show up empty-handed. Besides, she assumed that, like all the Conway girls, Amelia wasn't running short in the wine or cider department. One of the perks of being in the family business.

"Mom's recipe." Amelia smiled warmly, and if Britt didn't know better, she might say those were tears shining in her stoic sister's eyes. "I'll go set these up on my best tray."

Maddie lingered behind, frowning slightly. Britt licked her bottom lip, bracing herself for whatever Maddie was about to say. She got it. She had stayed away. Not called enough. Not visited. She'd paid the least amount of attention to Maddie.

"And here I thought that you'd be mad at me for carrying on Mom's recipes," Maddie surprised her by saying.

Britt blinked at her sister. Of all the things she could have come up with, this revelation was not one of them.

"Mad at you?" She replayed that first night in the kitchen, and later, at the dining table, where they also listened to Candy's stories while Maddie served the pie.

"You didn't seem very happy about me serving the pie that first night back," Maddie pointed out.

"You didn't seem very happy to see me the moment I walked into the kitchen."

"Because I was afraid of how you would react!" Maddie said, her eyes pleading, and for the first time since Britt had come back to town, she saw the emotion that her sister had been holding in all this time.

"I was…surprised," Britt admitted. She reached out and took her sister's hand, giving it a gentle squeeze. "In a good way. I never thought I'd taste that pie again. For just one moment, it was like she was there in the room with us." *Instead of Candy*, she thought darkly.

"But then at the market, you came straight up to me, asking all sorts of questions, like you were leading into something."

Britt now saw how everything could have been misread, and she grinned knowingly, preparing herself to discuss her ideas for those pies when there was a commotion in the hall and Amelia started calling out their names.

"Sounds like the birthday girl has arrived," Britt sighed, giving her sister a knowing smile. There would be another chance to talk. Maybe not later tonight. But soon.

"So you're not mad?" Maddie repeated, giving her a concerned look.

"I'm not mad," Britt repeated. "I'm…grateful."

And just as grateful in that moment for the huge smile that filled Maddie's face as she flung her arms around Britt's shoulders, just like she used to do when she was still a kid.

"Come on," Britt said, linking her arm. "Let's have some fun tonight."

Maddie nudged her playfully. "Fun in Blue Harbor? I wasn't sure you'd ever connect the two! Does that mean you'll come back again soon?"

Britt swallowed the knot in her throat. "I shouldn't have stayed away as long as I did," she said. And like everything about her past, that was one thing about her future that she was determined to never let happen again.

*

For the first night since he'd married Stephanie, Robbie was on his own. Keira had been invited to a sleepover, her first ever, and despite Robbie's misgivings about letting her go, Keira showed no such hesitation when he dropped her off at the Morrisons' cheerful house, with the promise to pick her up if she wanted to come home.

If Keira even heard, she didn't acknowledge it, and she'd forgotten to give him a hug goodbye too, instead taking her friend Lily's hand and scampering off down the hall, giggling in excitement.

"I'll pick her up in the morning," he said to Annette, who was thankfully happily married, with two kids and another on the way.

Annette gave him a reassuring smile. "She'll be fine."

Robbie had nodded. It was a lovely home, warm and inviting, and Keira would be fine, he was sure of it. The question was, would he be fine?

Not willing to go home and face a night alone in the house, he drove into town and joined the Friday night crowd at the inn. The pub was in full swing, as he expected it to be on a summer evening, especially once the rain started and the outdoor spots had to shut down their patios.

Jackson was behind the bar, right where he always

was, and despite knowing that was where he would be, Robbie felt an instant wave of relief at the sight of him. It was a reminder that he had made the right choice in coming back. That was at least one decision he could be sure of. The rest…the rest he couldn't be sure of anymore.

There were two spots open at the bar and he dropped onto one just as Natalie Clark dropped onto the other. He had an uncomfortable feeling that she'd followed him across the room.

"Don't see you in here much on weekends," she observed, flashing him a flirtatious grin.

"Keira's at a sleepover," he offered.

"My daughter's at the same one." Natalie grinned even wider. "Let's toast to that. Jackson?"

Jackson looked up and then glanced over at Robbie, who resisted holding up his hands to show that none of this was his idea.

"Two beers. Parents' night out."

Jackson slid the beers across the bar with a knowing look at Robbie but stepped away without a word. The crowd was too thick for him to jab Robbie right now. That part was coming, though. There was no doubt in Robbie's mind.

"Cheers," Robbie said, clinking her glass.

"A toast," Natalie corrected, eyeing him carefully. "To some…adult time."

Robbie cleared his throat. Yep, he shouldn't have let Keira go to that sleepover. He should be home with her, eating pizza and watching an animated movie.

He'd stay for the one beer and then get going. If An-

nette Morrison didn't call first, telling him that Keira wanted to come home.

"So what are your plans for tonight then?" he asked, hoping that she wouldn't misread his interest.

"It's my cousin Jenna's birthday." She wrinkled her nose. "Just us girls."

"Oh, right. Britt mentioned that," he said, taking a sip of his beer.

She gave him a funny squint of the eye. "I didn't realize that you and Britt were…talking again."

"Well, she's taken over her dad's place at the orchard." Temporarily, at least. But more and more he wondered if she was giving serious consideration to making things more permanent.

He took another sip of his beer, cooling that thought.

Natalie nodded silently, her look pensive. She took a long sip of her beer. "You were so tight growing up. Always thought you'd end up together."

Now it was his turn to nod silently. He took a long pull on his drink. "Yep."

"But I guess you moved on. And she did too. Childhood sweethearts," she mused, with a little laugh. "It's funny to think of the people we dated as kids."

There was nothing funny about it to him, and he'd more than dated Britt. He'd loved her. He'd been closer to her than his own brother, his best friends, even sometimes, he thought, his own wife.

Perhaps sensing that she wasn't going to get what she was looking for tonight, Natalie checked her watch and said, "Well, I suppose I should get over to the party before they send out a search patrol. But if you ever want to go in on a sitter together, just give me a call. It could be fun for the girls…and us."

She gave him a little smile, scooted off the barstool, and slipped away without another word.

Robbie glanced over his shoulder a moment later just to be sure she was gone. When he turned back to the bar, Jackson was right in front of him, flashing him a wicked grin.

"There's nothing going on there if that's what you're wondering," Robbie grumbled. He took a long sip of his beer. Maybe he would stay a little longer. Now that he was free to sit back and watch the game.

"I'm not used to seeing you here at night."

"Keira's sleeping over at a friend's house." Robbie frowned at his glass. "I'm guessing she'll be calling soon. Wanting to come home."

Jackson lifted an eyebrow. "Guessing? Or hoping?"

Robbie scowled at him. "What's that supposed to mean?"

Jackson sighed and flung a dishtowel over his shoulder. "I'm just saying that Keira is probably fine. More than fine."

Robbie knew that he was right. He'd witnessed her joy firsthand. "It's just…I want to protect her. I want to do what's best for her."

"And what's that?" Jackson asked pointedly. "Because it seems to me that what's best for you isn't necessarily what's best for Keira."

Under normal circumstances, Robbie might have shot

back at a comment like that, only tonight Jackson had homed in on the nagging suspicion that had been bugging him for days.

Ever since Keira met Britt.

*

After one and a half glasses of wine and an overflowing plate of Amelia's delicious appetizers, Britt was ready to call it a night. She'd caught up with her cousins—and their cousins—and promised Bella Clark to stop into the bookstore she now owned before she left town. The rain had let up, and if she made a dash for it now, she just might make it home without getting wet.

She carried her plate into the kitchen, where Natalie was uncorking another bottle of wine at the butcher block in the center of the room.

"You heading out already?" she asked.

Though they had known each other growing up, they'd never been close. Friendly and warm, mostly through their joint relation to Steve's daughters, but it stopped there. In fairness, the second half of high school had been a blur once Britt's mother was diagnosed, and other than her closest friends and sisters, the only person she'd spent much time with was Robbie.

Even then, Britt supposed she had started shutting the world out. She glanced at Natalie, thinking of how they might have been true friends if life had given her different circumstances.

Or if she'd responded to them differently.

But then, Natalie had her own troubles. A rocky marriage that quickly failed, leaving her to care for her daughter all on her own. A little girl who rarely—if ever—saw her father, from what Britt knew.

From the outside, Natalie was pretty and generous and full of life, but none of that could have been easy. She'd just chosen to handle it differently. For a moment, Britt wondered if she had handled it better. Natalie had rebounded, come home to her family when times got tough the way that Robbie had. Whereas Britt...Well, she'd walked away from her family, hadn't she?

"I'm thinking of slipping over to the Carriage House," Natalie continued, and despite it being a more popular spot in town, Britt picked up on something in Natalie's tone. "I was there earlier, actually. With Robbie."

Yep, there it was. Britt nodded and said nothing as she rinsed her plate in the sink, hating the way her heart was starting to pound. She'd been replaying last night every time she looked up from her work, thinking of the fun they'd had, the three of them in the kitchen, laughing at the mess, proud of their accomplishment. The way Keira had hugged her so tightly before she'd gone to bed.

The way that Robbie had almost kissed her.

"Our daughters are at a sleepover together," Natalie continued. She refilled her glass and took a sip. "It's not easy being a single parent. When you get a night out...Well, you make the most of it."

Britt glanced over at Natalie. "Is your daughter going to the party tomorrow?" she asked, kicking herself when she saw the surprise in Natalie's gaze that she was aware of the event. Robbie wasn't hers. He hadn't been in nearly

half a lifetime, but somehow she couldn't bear the thought of someone else being with him. Even someone as decent as Natalie, who had picked herself up after a bad marriage and was just trying her damn best, like the rest of them.

"She is," Natalie said, her eyes becoming cool.

Britt gave a tight smile. "I'll see you there, then."

Without another look at Natalie, she walked back into the living room to say goodnight to her cousins and sisters, who of course protested immediately that she couldn't leave.

"It's going to start raining again!" she insisted. But the truth was that right now she didn't care if she got wet—it seemed fitting, really. Almost deserved. Natalie was off to bond with Robbie in a way that she probably never could. And she was still pining after her high school boyfriend. Yep, there it was. No denying it.

"So? I'll drive you later," Amelia said. She held up her nearly full glass of wine. "I've barely had a glass. Better yet, you can stay here. I'm sure you can use a night away from Candy?" At this, the entire room burst into laughter, and even Britt found herself joining in.

Amelia's expression sobered when she glanced over Britt's shoulder. "You heading out already, Nat?"

Natalie feigned a guilty smile, but she was obviously happy with her decision to leave. "Girl time has been fun, but if I'm ever going to find Prince Charming, I have to go where the men are."

Or where Robbie was, Britt thought as her stomach rolled over.

"Have fun then!" Amelia said. Most of the other women sprang up from their seats to walk her to the door, leaving Amelia, Cora, and Maddie alone in the room.

"So. How's business at the holiday shop this time of year?" Britt asked Cora, but Amelia cut in.

"Uh-uh. None of that."

"None of what?" Now it was Britt's turn to feign innocence.

"Don't go changing the subject. You do know that Natalie has her eye on Robbie, don't you?" Amelia whispered, darting her eyes to the hall.

So there it was. Confirmed.

"I'm sure a lot of women in town have their eye on Robbie," Britt said lightly. "There can't be many options around here."

Cora shook her head. "Nope."

Britt had to laugh at her frankness. Still, the thought of Natalie with Robbie gnawed at her.

"She hasn't been shy about it," Maddie agreed. "I think she assumes that you wouldn't care, Britt."

"Of course I don't care!" Britt said, but she struggled to look up at any of her sisters, and with a shaking hand, she was pouring another glass of wine from the bottle on the coffee table. She'd take Amelia up on her offer and stay here for the night. Who knew? It might be fun.

Besides, she didn't fully trust herself not to take a detour past the inn, maybe take a glance through the window, see what was going on in the pub…

"If you're sure…" Cora said, and Britt looked at her sharply.

"Please. We were kids! We both moved on ages ago." She took a gulp of her drink, knowing that wasn't true. Robbie had moved on. Married. Had a child. Whereas Britt…she'd simply moved away.

"We could all go out," Amelia offered suddenly. "See what's going on with those two?"

Britt looked around at the effort Amelia had put into the party, from the trays of food, all handmade from scratch, to the candles that were slowly burning down to their wicks, and then around the room at her sisters, their faces each similar, but their personalities each so different.

She shook her head. Going where Robbie was tonight wouldn't change the past. It wouldn't change a thing. It was just too damn easy to get caught up in it—that's probably why Robbie had nearly kissed her last night. And stopped himself.

If Robbie was interested in Natalie, there was nothing she could do about it. She'd had her chance with him, a long time ago. And it hadn't been meant to be.

Like most things in life, romantic love was fleeting.

But her sisters, she thought, looking around the room, were a bond that couldn't be broken.

12

Keira's tea party was being held at the café, something that surprised Britt nearly as much as Amelia's failure to mention it to her.

"I wasn't exactly sure where you and Robbie stood with each other," Amelia said as they walked down the street together that morning—at the crack of dawn.

Amelia had failed to mention that sleeping over meant being awoken at the crack of dawn by the sound of the coffee machine percolating, and Amelia scrambling for the shower.

Britt had tossed the blanket from the sofa and sat up, bleary-eyed and dazed, to see her perky sister already dressed and sipping her first cup of the day.

"That's why I didn't drink much at the party." She winked.

Of course, Amelia told her to go back to sleep, not to mind her—she'd be at the café prepping for the breakfast crowd and getting a head-start on the decorations for the party. But at the thought of seeing Robbie today, Britt knew that there was no chance of going back to sleep.

She showered quickly, deciding to let her hair air-dry into loose waves the way she used to on lazy summer days, and joined Amelia on her quiet walk through town.

She loved seeing Blue Harbor like this, with the white-painted storefronts still dark, the sun just coming up and filling the sky with rosy hues, and the lake just behind the shops, slowly lapping at the rocky shore.

A few boats were already out on the water—the fishermen liked to get an early start, she knew. They passed the Carriage House Inn, and Britt stole a glance at the windows of the restaurant, even though she knew it was pointless. It was early morning and the place had been closed for hours. Whatever had happened last night after Natalie left the party was over and done with by now.

They turned at the next street, which led them right down to the water's edge, where the Firefly Café was tucked on the corner, just to the side of the harbor, on the water's edge. Amelia let them through the back door with a key and flicked on the lights, bringing the kitchen to light.

"I mean, one day you are in here barely speaking, and the next thing I know you're having coffee at a secluded table," Amelia continued. Clearly, she wasn't going to let it drop.

"That was for work," Britt said firmly.

"Was it?" Amelia said archly, but she gave a knowing smile.

"I'll have you know that we are both very vested in the success of the Cherry Festival this year," Britt said. "Speaking of which, would you host a stand? We want to expand things this year, bring in games and pony rides, and more food options, too." In the past, they just sold the wine and cider, cherry soda, brought in big popcorn and cotton candy machines, and offered cherry ice cream from the creamery in town.

Amelia looked hesitant, but there was a light of excitement in her eyes. "That's a big event."

"The biggest yet, if I have anything to do with it. I thought it might be nice to get all of us involved. And your food is exactly would really round out the day."

"The most food that I've ever done there were hot pretzels," Amelia said. "But I'm guessing you have something else in mind. And I do have more time these days, now that Candy is taking care of Dad."

Britt frowned at this. "I haven't thanked you yet, Amelia. And it's a long time overdue."

Amelia looked at her in surprise. "Thanked me?"

"For taking care of Dad. For going to college locally. For taking care of the house. For…for doing what I couldn't do."

Amelia gave her a little smile. "It wasn't entirely selfless. Taking care of everyone kept me busy. Kept my mind off things."

Britt sighed. "I understand that part." And without a job, she was putting everything she had into the orchard. "But you have a lot going on. It's okay if you're too busy for the Cherry Festival."

"Nonsense. I'm never too busy for my family," Amelia said, and Britt tried not to take that as a slight, knowing it wasn't meant to be one. "I'll put together a menu this weekend. Maybe I'll go with a cherry theme…"

"That's the spirit!" Britt mentally checked the item off her list. She hadn't looked this forward to a Cherry Festival since she was a kid and she knew that she could have all the pink cotton candy she wanted because her parents would be too busy to notice.

Grinning at the memory, Britt shook her head and tied on an apron. She wasn't much of a cook, but she could help her sisters as best she could. Maddie had the day off, Amelia had told her. Soon, Amelia's small staff would come in, but Britt could at least help set up for the party.

"Are these the decorations for Keira?" she asked, motioning to a few boxes of pink plastic teacups propped on a wooden chair.

Amelia nodded. "I'm setting them up in the front room. It's sunny in there, and we can push all the tables together. The party doesn't start until ten, but you may as well set up now. I know how things go and it will be too once we open to get that sort of thing done."

Britt took the cartons of party supplies into the front room and pushed the tables together, leaving one at the back of the room that Amelia would use to hold the presents and the cake.

After Amelia had prepped for the breakfast crowd, she came out to help. "Thanks for doing this."

"Thanks for letting me stay the night," Britt replied. She smoothed the tablecloth before setting out the plates. "The party was fun, too. It was nice to get my thoughts off things."

Amelia gave her a funny look. "Things? Or...Robbie."

Britt shook her head, but she couldn't fight her smile. "It's the business I'm worried about, actually." Sensing the alarm in her sister's eyes, she said, "It's not going to go under or anything like that." Not yet, anyway. "It's more that…well, it could certainly use a little boost."

"The farm isn't another of your clients, Britt. Dad isn't expecting you to go the extra mile."

"I'm actually thinking that it's exactly what he wants," Britt said, against her better judgment.

Amelia frowned as she tied more pink balloons to the back of a chair. "Is there a problem with the farm?"

Britt blew out a breath. With the café opening for business soon, it wasn't the time to be getting into a deep conversation, but she hadn't found as much time to connect with her sister as she would have liked.

"Not a problem that can't be fixed," Britt said brightly. She sloughed off the concern on her sister's face with a shrug. "You know me. Always looking for ways to improve operations."

"And you know Dad. Always looking to keep things the same."

"Until now," Britt said. "He's moved on, Amelia." There was a lump in her throat that she knew shouldn't be there. If her father wanted to move on and find happiness, then who was she to stop him? Her mother was gone, and nothing could bring her back. And no matter how far she ran or how long she stayed away, there was no escaping that fact.

Amelia nodded. "It was bound to happen eventually."

"I never thought it would happen." Maybe Britt had been naïve, or maybe she was just in denial.

"Never thought it would happen, or never wanted it to happen?" Amelia asked pointedly. "And Dad knew that."

Shame flooded Britt's cheeks as she stared at her sister. "But that's not the reason..." She blinked as her mind replayed the years since her mother's death at high speed. He'd never mentioned dating. Never talked about a desire to find someone else. He'd never even said that he was lonely.

Amelia shook her head. "No, I don't think it's the reason. Not the only one, at least. He didn't want to hurt us. And I don't think he was ready for any more change."

"And he's ready now," Britt said, emphasizing her earlier comment. "And not just about his social life."

Amelia looked at her in confusion. "What do you mean?"

Britt knew that Amelia could be trusted with this information. That she wouldn't pressure her one way or the other, but listen, and give an opinion only if it were asked for. And the truth of the matter was, Britt was asking for it. She needed it. She needed someone to tell her what to do because the choices she'd made for herself hadn't panned out the way she had wanted. She may be great at picking up the pieces of a struggling business, but when it came to her own life, she was hopeless.

"He wants me to take over the running of the business."

Amelia's eyes popped. Finally, she said, "He wants to retire?"

Britt nodded. "And he wants me to take his place."

Amelia blew out a breath. "Wow." She stared at the table of decorations, the pink plates and matching pink cups. A little menu card had been set up at each place setting. It would be a high tea complete with hot cocoa.

"What did you say?" Amelia finally asked.

Britt shrugged. "I didn't really know what to say. Coming back to Blue Harbor was only supposed to be temporary."

"But?" There was hope in Amelia's eyes, and Britt wasn't sure if she should snuff it out, or see it for what it was, and let it be the opinion that guided her.

Her family wanted her. And she had no real reason to stay away anymore.

But did she have a good enough reason to come back, she wondered, as Robbie appeared in the door.

*

By ten-thirty, the table was filled with ten little girls, the corner table was stacked high with presents in pink wrapping paper, and so far at least three cups of hot chocolate had spilled all over the table.

Robbie looked downright flustered as he tried to mop up the latest spill while keeping a more eager child from helping herself to a fifth pink mini cookie.

Britt saw the panicked look in his eyes and stepped forward with a roll of paper towels she had snagged from the kitchen. "Let me help," she said, expecting a protest and finding none.

Instead, Robbie stepped back wearily and gave her a sincere thank you when she promptly cleaned the spill, refilled cups, and advised the children that they were allowed three treats each because there was still ice cream and cake coming. She had the distinct impression that Natalie had hoped to be playing helper this morning, but after catching her eye, she'd been sure to announce that she had a yoga class to get to across town.

"How did you do that?" Robbie asked, a little breathlessly. "You make it look so easy."

"Don't forget that I'm the oldest of four girls. This was just a typical Sunday night dinner in my house growing up."

"Well, I'm glad you're here," he said, giving her a little smile. Their eyes locked, and for a moment, she dared to think that maybe he was grateful for more than the extra set of hands.

"I couldn't say no to Keira," Britt said with a shrug. She looked over at the birthday girl, who was seated at the head of the table, wearing a sparkly crown. "She's a really good kid, Robbie."

He seemed to stiffen for a moment. "I hope she's having a good time."

"Are you kidding me?" At that moment, another girl spilled her hot chocolate and the entire group broke into a fit of giggles. "She's having the time of her life."

He set a hand on her arm as she reached for the paper towels again. "Let me. I feel bad for getting you roped into this."

"Roped into what?"

He gave her a knowing look as he sopped up the mess, and she bit her lip to hide her smile. It was true that she hadn't exactly been expecting to stand at the edge of the room and monitor ten rambunctious seven-year-olds. But what had she been expecting? Something civilized and relaxing? A club chair and a glass of wine? Though that would be nice around now, especially when the squealing started and all the girls tried to talk over one another as if in a competition to see who could speak the loudest.

"You're way more of an adult than I am," she told Robbie with a sigh.

He let out a laugh, a bark really, that showed he didn't agree with her. "I'm glad I'm fooling someone because I'm not fooling myself." He sighed and frowned across the room at his daughter. "It's not easy being a single parent."

Natalie had given off the same sort of impression, and Britt wondered if this bonded them in a way that she could never understand or relate.

She thought of her own father, left with three younger daughters when she fled the house. Was that the reason he had put his own happiness on hold? Because he was overwhelmed with the responsibility of raising his girls? She could have stuck around, helped, been there for him. And for her sisters. Especially, Amelia.

"Let me make this up to you," Robbie said, and before she could give an answer, he said, "Please. This is probably not how you wanted to spend a day off."

"Yes and no. Keeping busy is good for me. It's what I do best."

"Meet me for a drink later?" His eyes latched with hers for a moment before looking away. "God knows I'll need one," he muttered, and she laughed.

"At the pub?"

"The dock?" he countered.

The dock. It was their usual spot. Their place, she

might have said once. Unsure of what he was getting at, or even how she felt about it, she sucked in a breath and nodded just once before he shot up his arm, waving at someone behind her.

She turned to see his parents, standing in the doorway holding a large, pink box tied with an oversized bow, looking completely bewildered by the shrill buzz in the air, and the energy that only a gaggle of little girls could cause.

"Daddy, I have to go to the bathroom," Keira said, coming over to take his hand.

Robbie glanced apologetically at his parents and back to her. "Be right back."

Britt smiled shyly at Robbie's mother, who was watching her from the doorway. Her husband had already disappeared into the main room of the café, no doubt looking for an escape from the high-pitched noise.

"It's good to see you, Britt," Bonnie said warmly. She gave her a hug like she always did, and even now, she felt achingly familiar.

Britt swallowed the lump in her throat. She'd always been close to Robbie's mother. Always felt bad about never saying goodbye when she'd left. But she'd been tired of saying goodbye by then. It felt too permanent. And she couldn't take any more certain loss.

"It's good to back," she said, surprised to realize that she meant it.

"How is your father doing?" Bonnie asked, edging closer to her. She still had the same kind eyes, but there were deeper lines in the corners now.

"He's…" Britt inhaled sharply, knowing that she needed to be honest with herself. "He's doing better than he has in years."

Bonnie blinked in confusion. After all, the man had fallen off a ladder and broke two bones. But then she seemed to process the meaning behind Britt's statement and gave a smile. "I'm sure having you here is all the medication he needs."

That and a caretaker who didn't mind wearing her shirts a little low cut, Britt thought with a little smile.

"So, you think you'll be staying in town then?"

"My plans are up in the air," Britt replied honestly.

Bonnie nodded slowly. "Just…don't break his heart again," she finally said, and it took a moment for Britt to realize that she wasn't talking about Britt's father. "He'd never admit it, but he waited for you to return until we all had to tell him you weren't coming back. Never seen him so sad. Couldn't stand being left behind, and so…off he went."

Britt stared at the woman for a moment, knowing a warning when she saw one, and knowing that she should heed it as best that she could.

13

Britt thought about Bonnie's words as she changed into jeans and a tank top and slipped her feet into flip-flops. Remembering how chilly the evenings were around here, she grabbed a cardigan from her drawer. Hardly date attire, but this wasn't a date, was it? It was two friends, meeting up, at the one place in all of Blue Harbor that held special meaning for the two of them.

Surely, that wasn't why Robbie had chosen it. He had probably picked it out of lack of anywhere else to go unless they wanted to go out in public and invite further speculation.

Or back to his house, where he'd almost kissed her. Because that's what he had nearly done, she was sure of it. Just as sure as she was that he'd pulled away, thought the better of it.

Just as sure that she shouldn't be wishing that he hadn't.

All this time, she'd assumed he'd moved on, without a look back, as easily as she claimed to have done. But it wasn't true at all. For either of them. He'd cared. Maybe he even still cared.

God knew she did. There was no denying it anymore.

She kept her hair down in the loose, carefree waves,

free of the tight knot that had defined her look for most of her professional life, and which had extended, without notice, into her personal life, too, much like her rigid ways had slipped through the cracks, infiltrating every facet of her life until she was so regimented, so careful about everything, that she no longer knew how to be spontaneous.

And tonight was anything if not spontaneous.

He was waiting for her when she arrived by bicycle fifteen minutes later. The sun was low in the sky and the water seemed to capture the last of its rays, causing it to sparkle. In the distance was Evening Island, and around it, only water, for as far as the eye could see.

Robbie was sitting on a folding chair, and another that he must have brought with him was empty at his side. The dock was lit at either end by a lantern, but she still depended on the dusk sky to be her guide as she crossed the wood planks until she reached him.

She was surprised to see that he had a bottle of wine and two glasses waiting for her.

"I told you I needed a drink after that party," he warned her when he caught her eyeing them.

She laughed and sank into the chair beside him. "I'm not complaining. I'm not used to being around children."

"Neither am I, really," Robbie said as he filled her glass and passed it to her. "It's different with Keira. We know each other's ways. We know how to live together. We're our own little team, I guess."

"That sounds nice." She gave a small smile and watched as he poured himself a glass before carefully setting the bottle down on the ground between them.

"You ever think about having kids?" Robbie asked her as he settled back in his seat.

She let out a nervous laugh. "My job hasn't exactly left time for me to have much of a social life."

"But you don't have that job anymore," Robbie reminded her.

It was true, and this time, when she thought of it, she no longer felt the sting of rejection or the panic of her blank future. Now, for the first time in a long time, she saw options.

Or at least possibility.

She pulled in a breath, kicking herself for feeling the need to even say what was nagging her all night and day. "I hear you were over at the pub last night," she said. When he gave her a quizzical look, she explained, "Natalie left the party to find you."

He rolled his eyes skyward, telling her everything she needed to know, and the relief that rushed over her confirmed what she already knew. She still cared about him. Maybe she had never stopped.

"I saw Natalie before the party. Chatted a bit." He gave her a long look. "If she came looking for me, I was long gone by then."

So he hadn't been waiting around for her, hadn't agreed to meet up after the party.

Well. Good.

"Did you have fun?" she asked, slanting him a glance.

"At the pub?" He let out a short laugh. "No. Not my scene anymore. I'd rather be home. With my family. With Keira," he clarified.

"I hear she went to a sleepover." When Robbie looked surprised, she elaborated. "Natalie told me that too."

"She did go to a sleepover. Not that I can say I was as pleased about it as Keira."

"It can't be easy to let her go."

"It will be worse when she's eighteen!" Robbie said, his eyes rounding in wonder.

Britt pushed back the guilt that had resurfaced. "I feel bad. For my dad. For leaving him the way I did. And then I get mad that he's moved on. That he's with this…Candy woman now."

Robbie started to chuckle and she swatted him. "I'm sorry. It's just…"

"I know," Britt said ruefully. "He sure waited long enough. And then he falls for this woman…who couldn't be more different than my mother." Tears burned the back of her eyes, and she couldn't blink them away. "I miss her so much. Even now, after all this time. And I can't stop thinking, is this what she would have wanted? Did I fail her somehow?"

Robbie leaned forward in his chair until she could see the fine features of his face. With the pad of his thumb, he brushed a tear from her cheek. "Your mother would have wanted you to be happy. And your dad, too. She wanted that house to be filled, with love, and laughter, and family. She loved her life here."

"You mean, she would have wanted me to stay instead of running off to Chicago?"

Robbie hesitated. "I think she would have wanted you to know that you can always come home."

Britt gave him a sad smile, knowing that he was right.

"Your mother loved traditions. The decorations she put out every year for Christmas. Her big holiday meals, where everyone was welcome. Those cupcakes that you made with Keira. Her pies. The orchard. Those things can still live on, Britt. They brought her joy. Those were the things that mattered to her. The traditions she passed down to her daughters."

"Thanks, Robbie," Britt said, pulling in a shaky breath.

She took a sip of the wine. It was cool and sweet, but there was something familiar about it, something that she couldn't quite place. "This is really good."

She glanced down at the bottle, but the darkness had fallen around them, and it was impossible to read the label.

"Thanks. I made it," Robbie said after a beat.

She stared at him. "You *made* this?" She took another sip. Of course! She could taste the familiar notes of Conway's blend, but there was something different about this wine, something she couldn't quite place. "But…I don't understand."

"It's just something I've been experimenting with, in my free time, of course," he added, in a rush, before they exchanged a smile. As if he could ever be in trouble with her. He could only ever be perfect to her. Then. Now. Always.

"Has my dad tried this?" she asked.

"I haven't run it by him yet," Robbie said with a shake of the head. "I didn't know if it was ready. You're actually the first person to have tried it."

"A blind taste test?" She laughed.

"More like the opinion that matters the most," he said, and even in the shadows of the low light coming from the lanterns, she could see the honesty in his eyes. And the hurt. All this time, she'd thought she was the only one who had missed what they'd once shared. But maybe she'd been wrong.

She'd been wrong about a lot of things.

"I like it," she said after taking another sip. "I like it a lot."

He gave a bashful smile and held up his glass. "I suppose we should toast."

There were many things she knew they could toast to. To her father's health. To the success of the Cherry Festival. To old times. To so many wonderful memories.

But there was only one thing that popped into her head at this moment. Only one thing that seemed fitting.

"To the future," she said, holding up her glass.

*

To the future. And what did that future look like, Robbie wondered. He hadn't dared to think about it lately. Once, when Stephanie was still with them, they talked about the future all the time. There was the eventual move to a bigger apartment that seemed to loom in the distance, something they casually discussed on Sunday mornings when they walked to brunch and passed open house signs. There was the unspoken assumption that there may be another child someday. There was talk of career plans—Stephanie wanted to have a storefront of

her own someday, and Robbie was working toward a promotion in a few years. There were vacations, destinations, places they wanted to visit, and discussions of holidays and school events and social plans.

Recently, Robbie didn't look beyond much more than next week. Oh, there were the little things, the responsibilities like summer camp for Keira, so she'd have something fun to do when school was out of session and he was working. And there was her birthday party, of course, and talk of a trip to Evening Island in a few weeks, because he'd given her a shiny new pink bike for her birthday and she was eager to ride a full lap around the island to show off her skills.

But beyond next week or next month, there was nothing, he realized. He hadn't thought to plan. Hadn't dared to dream.

And now, he couldn't help but think how it would be a month from now when Britt was gone again.

Or if she stayed.

Britt was leaning back in her chair, looking up at the sky, where the Milky Way swirled overhead. "Wow. I never stopped to really appreciate this until I stopped seeing it."

"Beautiful, isn't it?" He'd noticed it too, when he first moved back, away from the city lights that shielded the view. "Sometimes, when I look up like this, I wonder how I could have ever stayed away."

Britt nodded slowly. "Me too."

"You mean you'd really give up your city life for this?"

For this, he'd said. But what he'd really meant was: for me?

"I'm not renewing my lease," she said. "So it looks like I'll be here for the Cherry Festival after all."

"And after that? You mentioned the other night that you were considering staying in town."

Britt paused. "I'm a different person here than I am in Chicago. I thought that by leaving, I'd be happy. And I wasn't. My life…well, my life is pretty empty. And I think I made it that way."

His mouth tugged into a half-smile. "I can relate. When Stephanie died, I shut the world out. Focused on Keira, went through the motions."

"And now?" She was looking at him, earnestly, as if she really needed to know where he stood. Or maybe, where they stood.

"Now I think that I didn't realize how lonely we were." He swallowed hard. "I'm glad you're back, Britt."

She grew quiet for a moment, and they looked out onto the water, at the lights from the island in the distance. Finally, she turned to him. "Can I ask you something?"

He shrugged. "Shoot."

"Why'd you let me go? All those years ago, you didn't try to stop me."

He closed his eyes. He should have known that this would come up at some point, that the pain of their past couldn't be ignored forever.

"It wasn't my place to stop you, Britt," he said gruffly. "I wanted to, just as much as I wanted you to change your mind. I guess I thought that if you left, you'd come to your senses and come back. That you'd…miss me." There. He'd said it.

"I missed you every single day," she said quietly.

He blinked at her, shaking his head. "But you never came back. You never called."

"I was mad at you! For not coming with me. For letting me go."

"You needed to go. You wanted to go."

"And you wanted to stay," she said, the hurt in her voice as raw as the ache in his chest. "And then you left. Without me."

"I left because it didn't feel the same being in this town without you. I left because you never came back," he said firmly.

They fell into silence until she looked over and gave him a sad smile. "I guess we both did what we needed to do, then. Even if we were a little misguided."

He nodded. He hadn't dared to think about what might have been if he'd gone to college in Chicago with her, instead of staying in town, and then eventually moving to Boston. Meeting Stephanie. Having Keira.

He couldn't imagine a life without his daughter in it, and for that alone, he could have no regrets. But he did have a sense of loss. For the girl he'd once loved. The girl he now realized that he'd let down when she needed him the most.

"I'm sorry, Britt," he said, reaching out to take her hand.

She looked up at him, her eyes warm and kind, searching his as a small smile filled her face. "It was a long time ago. And I don't like thinking about the past."

"Maybe we don't have to. Maybe we can finally look forward."

Robbie swallowed the last of the hesitation that was holding him back, locked in the past, and leaned forward to close the distance between them. And then, he kissed her, slowly, as if it was their very first kiss even though it was probably their thousandth kiss, but this time he made it last, just a little bit longer, because just like the stars that shone above them, he hadn't truly realized how wonderful his life could be, until he'd found her again.

14

Britt had spent the better part of the next morning putting the final touches on the plans for the Cherry Festival, but she had spent all of last night thinking about Robbie's wine. When she wasn't thinking of the kiss.

The market was nearing its end when she came down from the office and crossed toward the barn, and despite the rain that had started early that day, she was pleased to see the parking lot so full, and the families coming out of the doors with their arms full of fresh fruit and the occasional pie box.

She smiled, thinking that Robbie was right. That her mother would be happy to know that the tradition was being carried on, even if she wasn't here to see it.

Britt swept her eyes over the room when she entered, not knowing exactly how she would react to Robbie when she saw him, and then made her way over to Maddie, who was closing up for the day.

"I was thinking that we should offer these pies at the Cherry Festival," she said.

Maddie looked pleased. "Sure! I mean, we've never done it before, but I could make a dozen or so cherry pies. Mom always made those for Dad's birthday."

Britt smiled at the memory. Their dad never wanted

cake, only pie for his birthday. Claimed it would be disloyal of him as an orchard owner otherwise.

"I was actually thinking of something bigger in scale," Britt explained. "This event pulls in a huge crowd. People come to Blue Harbor just for the festival weekend. It's a great opportunity to really increase profits, and your pies are a big seller." When Maddie didn't respond right away, Britt said, "We could do smaller pies, for individuals. We'd need at least two hundred, but more would be better. We can ask some of the staff to pitch in—"

Maddie's look stopped her. Her eyes were wide in disbelief, and her smile had long since slipped. "But that would require sharing Mom's recipe!"

Britt considered this for a moment, sensing Maddie's unease. "Yes. I suppose it would."

"But that's...That's..." Maddie seemed on the verge of tears. "That's Mom's recipe, Britt."

"And everyone loves her pies!" Britt said. "Don't you think that would make her happy?"

Maddie's shoulders slumped as she scuffed her shoe along the wood-planked floor. "I guess. I just..."

A noise cut through the barn. One that Britt hadn't heard in so long she'd forgotten the sound. It was her phone, ringing in her pocket. It hadn't occurred to her that for the entire time she'd been back in Blue Harbor, she hadn't felt the endless need to check her device the way she did when she was back in Chicago, or working at her old firm.

The orchard didn't require that kind of endless interruption. Things moved slower here. If you needed to talk to someone, you simply walked over to them.

She looked down at her phone, not recognizing the number. Stepping to the side where she could talk in private, she held it to her ear and answered.

"Britt Conway?"

She frowned. "Yes."

"This is Vickie Worthington." Immediately Britt knew the name from the job she'd interviewed for right before coming back to Blue Harbor. "I'm sorry to call you on a Sunday, but we'd like to bring you in for a second interview. We've had a sudden windfall of clients which is why we haven't contacted you sooner, and with all the new business, we're looking to fill the position by next week. Is there any chance you would be free to meet with us this Tuesday morning?"

Tuesday morning. The drive wouldn't be bad; she could leave tomorrow, check on her apartment, and be back in Blue Harbor by Tuesday night. She was planning to make the trip next weekend, anyway…to pack up her apartment. And return to Blue Harbor.

Only now she might not have to think about the return drive at all. They needed to fill the position immediately. She could start right away. Find another apartment. Or see if her landlord hadn't yet rented hers.

The timing was almost perfect, really. Her father was scheduled to return to work next week. She wasn't really needed here after that.

Except that wasn't true, she thought miserably as she looked back into the barn, where Maddie was beaming at a line of customers and Keira was helping Robbie line up jars of preserves.

She looked up at the sign advertising the Cherry Festival that Robbie must have hung up this morning. The event was now less than two weeks away. If she got the job, she wouldn't be here to see it through.

Or enjoy it.

"Hello? Do I still you have you?"

"I'm still here," Britt said quickly. She didn't have time to react, or think. There was an opportunity on the line, a reminder of the real life she had waiting for her back in Chicago. The career she had built. The path she had set in motion.

She was an adult now. A thirty-two-year-old woman with bills to pay and an apartment to rent, and a career that she had made all on her own. To walk away from it all now felt rash and emotional.

This was what she had wanted. The answer to her fears. Stability. Routine. A life with structure, not complication. Or risk.

"Tuesday at nine," she said into the phone, forcing a smile. "I'll be there."

She disconnected the call and sighed before stuffing the device back into her bag. She closed her eyes, told herself that it was just an interview, only she knew that it was much more than that.

It was a choice. A choice to pursue a life outside of Blue Harbor, away from this orchard. Her family.

And Robbie.

"Be where?" Robbie asked now, coming up beside her, and she wondered by the look in his eyes just how much he had heard. Or suspected.

She pulled in a breath, told herself that she was doing the right thing and that she couldn't hide it from him. She wouldn't be here tomorrow. Or Tuesday.

She wasn't sure if she'd be back at all.

"I just got a call about a job opportunity. In Chicago."

His jaw immediately stiffened. "I see."

"I interviewed with them once already," she explained. "Before I came back. It's…a good opportunity. More of what I was doing. I'd be…helping people. Well, companies. Helping companies. It's just a second interview." She was rambling, trying to convince him nearly as much as she was trying to convince herself. That she wanted this. That she was justified. That she hadn't led him on.

Hadn't let herself dare to wish for something different.

"So you're going to go?"

"I don't see much choice," she said, shrugging her shoulders. "I have bills to pay, just like everyone else."

"You always have a choice, Britt." Robbie's eyes were flat, his mouth a thin line of disapproval, and from the way he was looking at her, she suspected that he was holding back saying more.

"What's the alternative? To stay here and run this struggling orchard that might not be around another year if we get another bad crop?"

His jaw flinched. "So you'll help other businesses, but not your own?"

He'd hit her square in the chest and he knew it. "That's hardly fair, considering I've done nothing but come up with ideas to try to improve this place. Ideas that you haven't exactly supported."

"Like cutting loyal staff? Or mass producing your mother's pies? You're right, Britt. I don't support those ideas, and I doubt your father would either."

"Oh, he's just stubborn—" But it was true, she knew. There was no way that Dennis Conway would let go of people who had worked this land and bottled his wine for thirty years or more. Instead, he'd take out a loan, as he had done. A loan he would now struggle to repay.

"No, you're stubborn, Britt," Robbie shot back. She couldn't remember ever seeing him so angry. Or so hurt. "You made up your mind about this town a long time ago, and I should have seen that. You left, and you left your heart behind when you did."

She flinched at the harshness of his tone. "It's just an interview."

"It's not just an interview and you and I both know that," he said. He shook his head, running a hand through his hair. "You're looking for another reason to leave. You want to leave."

"I don't know what I want!" she all but shouted, stunned at her own omission.

He looked at her sadly and nodded his head. "Well, I do. And I should have stuck to that. Do me a favor and stay clear of Keira today. I don't her need her getting any closer to a woman who's just going to leave her again."

The warning was like a slap to her face. "You know I'd never do anything to hurt Keira," she said.

"And me?" he asked, his eyes dark with hurt.

Maybe it was justice. Maybe she deserved it.

But it wasn't what she had wanted.

"I need to focus on my future," she said to him.

"And here I thought I might be in your future this time." He backed up, away from her, and this time, she knew that it was him leaving her before she had a chance to do it first.

*

The house was quiet when Britt returned a short while later. Her dad, she imagined, was napping in his study, as he usually did when a ballgame was on. Woke up just in time to see the final score and give a big reaction.

Candy's car was mercifully gone. The last thing that Britt needed right now was to explain her mood or turn her head if Candy tried to cram one more of those cheese biscuits into her firmly closed mouth on her way out the door each morning.

Her knuckles hovered over the closed door to her dad's study. In many ways, having this conversation would be worse than the one she'd just had with Robbie. She would be letting him down. And worse, she'd be letting Conway Orchard down.

She hadn't managed to save it. She wouldn't be here to see the Cherry Festival and all her ideas for it through to completion. The loan may not get paid off, not if they had another rainy season this fall. And who would her father sell the orchard to? Who would take care of it as she would have? Robbie would do a good job, but he wasn't family. And maybe, that was all her doing.

All these thoughts swarmed her mind as she rapped on the wood, so lightly that she wasn't even sure her father would hear, and to her dismay he did, calling her in. There was no going back now.

"Hi Dad," she said as she came into the room. The windows had been cracked, and the breeze off the lake gave the space a fresh, airy feeling. On the windowsill was a vase full of fresh sunflowers, and on the bed was a new blanket in a handsome shade of beige.

"Candy bought it for me," he explained when he saw her eyeing it.

"Oh." Britt hadn't expected that. "Well, that was…nice of her."

Dennis pursed his lips but said nothing more. He picked up the remote and gestured to the television housed in the sturdy armoire. "Game's about to start if you care to join me."

She'd never been into the sports he cared about, but she often joined him just the same, for the company, usually with a book in her lap. Her mother used to pass by the open door and give her a little wink from the hallway.

Britt had taken good care of her father at one point in time. When had she stopped? And could she really stop now?

She opened the top drawer of his desk. He'd never minded her rifling through his things, which she supposed was why he didn't mind her having full access to his files at work. The top drawer was full of the same pens and notepads he'd always stashed away, a random rubber band, an envelope of stamps. The right-side drawer held old albums—ones that she now couldn't bear to look through. And the left-side drawer…

Her breath caught when she saw the faded, folded cotton apron, its strings tied in a neat bow.

"Mom's apron," she said, looking at him quizzically. She'd assumed that Amelia had taken it with her to the café, or to her house.

"Amelia put it there," her father said knowingly. "Not sure that's the best place for it, but I trust we'll figure that out in time."

Britt ran her hand over the fabric and closed her eyes. For a moment she was still just nine years old, wrapping her hands around her mother's waist, the very same fabric so familiar under her fingertips.

She blinked away the tears and closed the drawer gently.

"Can I ask you a question, Dad?" she blurted, not even sure why she needed to know, but suddenly finding that she did. Badly. There were so many unanswered questions, emotions that hadn't been voiced because they'd each been trying to protect the other.

"Anything," he said, fumbling with the remote.

"Why did you want me to take over the orchard? I haven't been back in fourteen years. Why would you want me?"

He set his hand down and stared at her, his expression folding into one of complete surprise and tenderness. "My girl, why wouldn't I want you? Who else could pass down the Conway family traditions as you have?"

"But Amelia and Maddie—"

"Oh, Maddie's carrying down the traditions in her own way, with the pies, of course. And Amelia's running a successful operation over there. She learned that cooking from your mother. And Cora. She loves Christmas even more than your mother, and that woman didn't even want to take the tree down until all the needles had fallen off." He chuckled at the memory until his smile turned sad. "But you, Britt, you loved that orchard. Maybe even more than I ever did. God knows you'd probably do a better job running it."

"I know about the loan," Britt said. It was easier, talking about facts, about finances, and business than everything else. But her heart was hammering and her eyes were clouding and she couldn't let go of what he'd said, because it was true. She had loved that orchard. It was every bit her home that this house ever was.

Dennis waved his hand through the air. "We've had some better years than others. I know what works. I know what doesn't."

She waited for him to say that this was why things should never change.

Instead, he surprised her by saying, "But you know the heart of that place, Britt. And I think you alone would know how to make everyone see how special it is, not just this family. It's not all about profit, I've learned. It's about the people. And the traditions. That's what mattered to your mother, and to me. And I can't see anyone else carrying on that legacy other than you."

Legacy. The word hit something deep inside her, tugging at a possibility. Tapping at a purpose.

Britt swallowed hard, trying to take it all in. What her father was saying was true. She could make people see

how special Conway Orchard was. She could make the business everything it was meant to be. And the money her mother had left her—the money she had saved for just the right reason—could save it. Carry it on.

But what her father was telling her was that the business was never meant to be a huge financial success. It was meant to be authentic, and honest, and hard-working, and small. Something you stood by, through the good years and the bad years. Something that could be passed down and carried along. Like the pies that Maddie baked, not because she cared how many she sold, but because she cared enough to keep that special recipe alive.

"Can I ask you another question, Dad?" She looked from the blanket on his lap to the flowers in the window, to the little stack of inspiration sticky notes attached to the edge of his TV tray. "Do you miss Mom?"

His eyes were sharp on hers. "Every damn day," he whispered.

"I'm happy that you found someone, Dad," she said, reaching out to take his hand. "I just hope you didn't turn away from love because of me."

"Your mother was one of a kind. Just like the four of you girls. No one is looking to replace her, Britt. And for a long time, I never thought I could fill that space in my heart reserved for her." He sighed. "Then one day, I realized, I didn't have to. There's room in here for whatever we choose to let in."

Britt gave her father a watery smile. Whatever we choose to let in, she repeated to herself.

For far too long, all she could think about was what

she could push out, but today, she had a second chance to change that. And there weren't many second chances in life, were there?

15

That night, Robbie took Keira over to the inn for a Sunday night dinner with his parents and brother—something they tried to do once a month since he'd come back to town and usually stuck to, especially since Tony in the kitchen always cooked them the fish and chips that had been every bit the staple of his childhood that his mother's holiday turkey dinners had been. It was part of Robbie's effort to establish a routine for Keira more than anything, and she wasn't shy about telling him just how much she looked forward to these nights, even if at first Robbie had dreaded the social effort, even with his own family.

Soon, though, the conversation and company was a bright spot on the calendar for both of them—a chance for him to break away from his own solitude and comfort, and a chance to relax, and even laugh. Once again, his daughter had shown him that what he wanted was best for him was what made her happy—even if he didn't see that at first.

Keira was happiest being around other people. Letting life in, rather than hiding from it.

And right now, it would be so easy to hide again. To shield himself from the pain. To try to protect her from it.

Britt was leaving. Keira would be disappointed, but she would bounce back.

And he...he supposed he should have known this would happen. That he shouldn't be feeling all the anger and disappointment that had plagued him all day.

Tonight, even the idea of Tony's fish and chips couldn't entice him, and the thought of sitting at their usual round table in the restaurant of the inn, pretending like everything was okay, was almost worse than the thought of being home, alone once Keira went to bed, replaying the events of the past few weeks over and over.

But if there was one thing that his time with Britt had taught him, it was that being alone was worse than opening himself up again. And it certainly wasn't what was best for Keira. Besides, she'd reminded him no less than six times that tonight there was a hot fudge sundae on the menu—something that Robbie knew Tony added to the Sunday night specials specifically because Keira always asked for one.

Jackson was the first person Robbie saw when he walked in—sitting at their usual table near the hearth—his night off from the bar. Robbie braced himself for the teasing that his brother could never seem to resist, knowing that word traveled fast in this town and would have probably made it all the way to these walls by now. He couldn't have been more relieved when he saw his mother walk into the room before he had taken a seat. Keira could always be relied on to hold court for the beginning of these family meals, and as usual, they were all happy to listen to her share the details of her week.

A PLACE FOR US

Robbie waited to see if Britt's name would be mentioned, and was happy to see that it was not.

He took a sip of his iced water. One hurdle cleared. But there would be more.

They had barely placed their orders when Jackson grinned and said, "Natalie Clark came back the other night looking for you."

Robbie pretended to be unaware of this and tried to shrug it off, but there was no denying the light in his mother's eyes. He stifled a groan and glanced at his daughter, but Keira was coloring in a book, tuned out of the conversation.

"Don't get your hopes up too much, Mom," Jackson was the one to warn. "If you ask me, Robbie still has his sights set on Britt."

So Jackson didn't know about Britt then. But it wouldn't be long before he did. Before they all did. Best to end this right here and now.

Robbie licked his lower lip, knowing that he could shut this conversation down with a simple statement of fact, but he didn't want to say it in front of Keira.

"Daddy," Keira said, looking up. "I have to go to the bathroom."

He pushed his chair back, happy for an excuse to leave the table, but this time she just grinned and said, "I can find it by myself. I know the way."

"It's practically her second home," his dad pointed out.

Robbie sat back down, watching as his little girl skipped across the dining room to the back hallway. She was growing up. She was showing her independence. She was showing him that she would be okay.

"Britt's leaving town," he said firmly, not meeting anyone's eye. There. That should do it. No more hints. No more teasing. Couldn't they just eat in silence for a change? Talk about the weather? Or the business at the inn? Some difficult guests had surely checked in since their last meal together—someone who could perhaps top last month's story about the guest who asked for twelve pillows for reasons they never knew?

He waited for his mother's groan of disappointment, or maybe even some shame in his brother's eyes for once.

Instead, when he looked up, he saw that every member of his family was staring at him expectedly.

Finally, his mother spoke. "And you're just going to let her go?"

He blinked in surprise. "It's her choice."

"But is it *really* what she wants?" Bonnie shook her head. "And what about what you want? Do you want her to go?"

Of course he didn't, but he couldn't say that, didn't even want to admit it to himself.

"It's not my decision to make," he said firmly. Britt was a grown woman. A woman who had chosen to pursue a career instead of love.

Or a woman who had chosen to run from her feelings—for the second time in her life.

Just like he had done. And maybe, just like he was doing now.

"It's your life, brother," Jackson said, giving him a

look of naked disapproval. "But you don't get many second chances, do you?"

Robbie stared at his brother's face, for once not teasing, his eyes flat, not full of mirth like usual, and despite himself, he cursed under his breath. "Damn it, Jackson. When did you get so smart?"

"Just looking out for my little brother," he said, back to his mischievous grin. "You know I always have your back, even if I give you a hard time."

Robbie knew it. They all did.

It was why he'd come home. Why he'd come to this dinner. And why he could never leave this town again.

And why Britt shouldn't either.

*

Britt awoke to the sun shining through her pink curtains, the quilt heavy on her body, and Candy's soprano floating up the stairs.

And despite the crack in Candy's voice when she tried to hit that last note, Britt was almost pleased for the sound of it.

Robbie had been right about what he said the other day. Her mother would have been happy to know that this house was not sitting empty. That it was once again filled with smiles and laughter and singing, however bad.

And she'd be happy to know that Maddie was carrying on the tradition of her pies, and that the lucky few who arrived early on market day to buy one would enjoy them at the dinner table later that night.

And what would her mother make of Britt's decision, she wondered, as she showered and dressed for the day.

But she didn't need to ponder that thought for long. She knew. In her heart of hearts, she had always known.

Her mother wanted what was best for her. What made *her* happy. It had just taken Britt a long time to know what that was.

Her suitcase was packed and ready, at the foot of her bed, and she loaded her toiletries into the tote bag she swung over her shoulder. Candy was standing at the stove when she arrived downstairs a minute later, and before Britt could even say good morning, Candy was thrusting a brown paper bag at her with a big grin.

"For the road," she explained. "In case you get hungry. No pressure."

Britt didn't need to look inside to know that they were Candy's "famous" cheese biscuits. She offered her first genuine smile to the woman who had brought her father such unexpected joy in the past few weeks, and a second chance at sharing his life with someone instead of living in the past.

"Thank you, Candy," Britt said. They were still warm, and from the smell alone, Britt knew she'd eat at least two before she'd even crossed the town line. But it wasn't just the breakfast that she was grateful for it. "For everything. You've…taken good care of my father. I'm not sure he even knew what he needed or what would make him happy until you came along."

Candy's cheeks turned pink as her smile bloomed. "Honey, no one knows what makes them happy until it shows up on the doorstep. And sometimes, it has to knock loudly. And ring the doorbell, if you get my drift."

She laughed merrily and Britt realized for the first time since arriving that it was a lovely, contagious sound.

"Well, I'd better go say goodbye to my father," she said with a sigh.

She walked down the hall to the study and poked her head around the door. Her father was scratching at the inside of his arm cast with a ruler.

"This thing can't come off soon enough!" he complained.

"End of the week, right?" Britt marveled at how quickly the time had passed. "Then it's back to normal."

From the kitchen, Candy was breaking out in song again. Dennis skirted his eyes to the door and back to her, hiding his smile. "Maybe not completely back to normal."

Britt grinned. "It's a long drive. I should probably get going."

"You be safe," her dad said, accepting the ginger hug she offered him.

"I should be telling you that," she joked. Britt couldn't help but still worry about injuring him worse, but he was a strong man, she knew. Stronger than she'd known. "I'll call you to let you know when I arrive."

"I'll be here," he replied as he reached for the ruler again.

Britt lingered in the doorway, clutching the warm bag of biscuits, watching her father with a full heart, knowing that he would be right here. And that he wouldn't be alone.

Her bags were at the foot of the stairs where she'd left them, and she opened the front door to carry them out to her car—and came face to face with Robbie Bradford.

"Robbie." She stared at him, not sure why he would be here unless her father had called him over to discuss business matters.

He glanced down at the suitcase in her hand and back up at her. "Do you have a minute to talk?"

She hesitated. She had hoped to be getting into Chicago before rush hour traffic hit in the midafternoon. But seeing the way his forehead pinched where his brows met, she couldn't refuse him.

She set the suitcase down at her feet and closed the front door behind her. For a second, she had a flashback of standing on this very same porch with Robbie when they were younger, and he would walk her to the front door after their dates, give her a kiss goodnight. Sometimes a kiss that felt like it could last until the next morning.

"I didn't try to stop you from leaving last time. I didn't try to change your mind. But I'm here to change it now, Britt. If you'll give me the chance."

She opened her mouth, but he shook his head. "Please. I need to say this."

She nodded. "Okay."

"After Keira's mom died, I tried to shut out the world. And I came back here, and I saw that I didn't have to be alone. That there are people who care if you let them." He reached out and took her hand. "And I care, Britt. About you. And I know that I've been happier in these past couple of weeks than I have been in a long time. And Keira's been happier too. And I think if you stopped and

thought about it, you'd know that you were happier here, Britt. I know you. I know you."

Hot tears burned in her eyes, and she couldn't blink them away if she tried. "You do know me. Everyone here does. And you were right, that I have been happier back in Blue Harbor than I ever was one day in Chicago. Or on the road. No one knew me, or what I'd been through, and I thought that would be easier somehow. But it wasn't."

"Then why go?"

"I have to go," she said slowly. She gave him a small smile. "Because I have to pack up my apartment before the new tenant moves in next weekend."

He frowned, trying to understand. "You mean…you're staying?"

She nodded. "You said something yesterday that I needed to hear. I sacrificed a lot when I left this town all those years. I left my sisters, my father, my friends, and neighbors. The orchard. But most of all, I left my heart behind, because my heart belonged with you. And it still does, Robbie."

He pulled in a breath and looked down at her, a little smile quirking the corner of his mouth.

"You know, I think it was right here on this very porch where we had our last kiss before I left town."

He tipped his head, grinning now. "Who said it had to be our last kiss?"

"Not me," she said. "And I'm hoping that's not what you want either."

"All I ever wanted was for you to stay in Blue Harbor,

Britt," Robbie said, as he reached down and took her hands. "Then, and now." Still, his eyes were questioning. "So you're really staying?"

She smiled up at him as he leaned down to kiss her. "There's no place I'd rather be."

epilogue

The Cherry Festival was everything that Britt could have hoped it would be: the sun was shining in a bright blue sky, and the entire town had turned out for the event within the first hour of the day. It was a larger event than usual, but that didn't make it any less personal.

Maddie had made an extra dozen pies—and already sold them to eager locals. Amelia was assisted at her food stand by Cora, and even Candy had been put to use manning the cotton candy machine, something she seemed to take more joy in than the children, as she swirled the paper sticks through the pink confection.

"As sweet as Candy," she laughed happily each time she handed over the treat.

Britt caught her dad's eye and saw the little smile he couldn't hide. Candy would never be their mother, and in many ways, she couldn't be more different. And maybe, that was for the best. It was certainly what was best for Britt's father.

"I have to hand it to you," Dennis said as he slowly moved toward her on his crutches. His arm cast was off and his leg would be healed in time to enjoy some long summer walks along the lakefront—something that Candy kept hinting at, though she insisted on using the term "romantic stroll."

"Dad—be careful. Here, let me get you a chair."

Her father gave her a reproachful look. "Stop fussing over me, Britt. I have Candy doing enough of that already."

And loving every minute of it, she thought ruefully.

"But Dad—"

He held up a hand, steadying himself against the weight of his crutches. "If you want to feel like you're helping me, then look around you. This is the biggest turnout we've ever had, and raffling off a monthly case of wine was a brilliant idea."

"Speaking of wine, did you try our new blend?"

It was Robbie's blend really, but Britt had been the one to insist he name it in traditional Conway fashion: after his daughter.

"Might be the best one yet." Dennis grinned. "I'm excited to see what you'll do with the place."

"You aren't afraid of the changes?" she asked nervously.

"Life is full of changes, honey," Dennis said to her. "Some are just easier than others."

Britt gave her father a squeeze and spotted Maddie heading into the barn, where the extra supplies were housed. Seizing her chance, she quickened her pace after her youngest sister, calling out her name until Maddie turned around.

"I have something for you." Britt walked behind the market counter, where she'd stashed the gift. It was wrapped in tissue paper and tucked inside a cheerful yellow bag, but seeing it now, she knew it didn't require anything more than what it was.

Carefully, she pulled her mother's apron from the paper and stood.

Maddie let out a small gasp. When she looked back up at Britt, her eyes had welled with tears. "Mom's apron."

"*Your* apron," Britt said. "It should have been yours all this time."

"But Amelia's the one with the café," Maddie protested, but Britt shook her head.

"You're the one who has kept Mom's recipes alive all this time. You're the one who has made these pies, and loved every second of it, just like she did."

"Britt—I've thought a lot about what you said. About the pies—"

Britt shook her head. "I've thought a lot about it too. And you were right. That recipe wasn't meant to be shared. It was meant to be carried on. And that's exactly what you're doing." She held the apron out farther. "You're doing exactly what Mom would have wanted. I know she would have been happy."

"I never dared to wear it before." Maddie reverently took the apron into her hands and smoothed down the worn, cotton fabric. "I'll take good care of it."

Britt gave her hand a squeeze. "I know you will."

She walked away, out into the sunshine, taking in the fields all around her with a satisfied sigh. Out in the distance, people were already picking baskets of cherries, and Dory was telling everyone how to spot the ripest fruit, albeit with a tad too much detail.

Robbie caught her eye and grinned, and she moved through the crowds until she'd reached him. Keira's face was already painted like a ladybug, and she had an ice cream stain down the front of her white eyelet dress.

"This is the best day ever!" Keira exclaimed as soon as Britt was in earshot, and she had to agree, it was.

"It all came together," she said, looking at the scope of the festival, the crowds gathered at the picnic tables, the children engrossed in their games. "Or maybe I should say everyone came together."

"You still happy with your decision?" Robbie asked as they turned toward the fields and the rows and rows of grapes and over to the cherry trees and apple trees that extended as far as the eye could see.

"I guess I still can't believe that I'm here." She sighed happily.

"This place was always meant to be yours, Britt."

She shook her head and gave his arm a squeeze. "No. It was meant to be ours."

"And will it someday be mine?" Keira asked excitedly, separating their bodies, only to join each of their hands.

Britt caught Robbie's eye and shrugged. "You never know. Life is anything but predictable."

"And you're okay with that?" Robbie asked, looking over Keira's head at her as they walked back toward the festival, swinging the little girl between them. "There will be good years and bad years."

"And we'll get through it," she said. "Together."

ABOUT THE AUTHOR

Olivia Miles is a *USA Today* bestselling author of feel-good women's fiction with a romantic twist. She has frequently been ranked as an Amazon Top 100 author, and her books have appeared on several bestseller lists, including Amazon charts, BookScan, and USA Today. Treasured by readers across the globe, Olivia's heartwarming stories have been translated into German, French, and Hungarian, with editions in Australia in the United Kingdom.

Olivia lives just outside Chicago with her family. Visit www.OliviaMilesBooks.com for more.

Made in United States
Troutdale, OR
06/19/2023

10665307R10130